SO-BBN-968

NIGHT GAME

Books by Alison Gordon

Fiction

The Dead Pull Hitter
Safe at Home
Night Game

Non-Fiction

Foul Balls: Five Years in the American League

NIGHT GAME

A KATE HENRY MYSTERY

A novel by

Alison Gordon

St. Martin's Press
New York

R0121607744
HUMCA

HOUSTON PUBLIC LIBRARY

NIGHT GAME. Copyright © 1992 by Alison Gordon.
All rights reserved. Printed in the United States of
America. No part of this book may be used or reproduced
in any manner whatsoever without written permission
except in the case of brief quotations embodied in critical
articles or reviews. For information, address St. Martin's
Press, 175 Fifth Avenue, New York, N.Y. 10010.

Library of Congress Cataloging-in-Publication Data

Gordon, Alison.
    Night game / Alison Gordon.
        p.   cm.
    ISBN 0-312-09062-5
    I. Title.
PR9199.3.G617N5   1993
813'.54—dc20   92-43170
                                                CIP

First published in Canada by McClelland & Stewart Inc.

First U.S. Edition: March 1993
10 9 8 7 6 5 4 3 2 1

All the events and characters in this book are fictitious. Any resemblance to persons living or dead is purely coincidental.

For the foreign correspondents:
women in the locker room.

ACKNOWLEDGMENTS

Thanks are due to Ken Carson; Sergeant Rick McBride of the Dunedin, Florida, Police Department; Lee Davis Creal; Kate Lazier; Ellen Seligman; Linda Williams; Norma Wilkie; the Gordon Family Manuscript Reading Service; and to Paul Bennett, who saved me from The Grapefruit Dead.

NIGHT GAME

CHAPTER

1

She minced across the infield on spike-heeled sandals, wearing jeans so tight that I wondered how she got out of them as often as she was reputed to. She wore an oversized white satin shirt tied around her tiny waist, and unbuttoned to show a red tube-top stretched to the ripping point by her enormous breasts. She stopped, pulled a comb out of her large canvas carry-all, and ran it through her shoulder-length, tousled, streaked blonde curls. When she saw me, she threw me a little-girl wave, fluttering her scarlet-tipped fingers in my direction. I pretended I didn't notice.

Three hours into my forty-second birthday, I was sitting in the Horkins Field stands, halfway down the right-field foul line, drinking lukewarm coffee from the media room, and feeling sorry for myself. I had no time for Juicy Lucy Cartwright.

We're not talking mid-life crisis here. Age has never been a difficulty for me. I would rather be my age than Lucy's twenty-two. On this particular day, my problem was that I was stuck in the god-forsaken retirement village of Sunland, Florida, with twenty column inches to fill for the next day's Toronto *Planet*, and I didn't have a clue what I was going to fill them with. Besides, after a winter of stunningly robust health, ten days into my exile among the palms and polyester, I had a stinking cold.

My brain had turned to ricotta cheese, my nose was red and runny, I couldn't hear for beans, and every time I lit a cigarette I coughed like Camille.

I lit another one, coughed, and tried to figure out how to get through the day. My job, senior baseball writer for the *Planet*, is dependent upon the guys who play for the Toronto Titans baseball team. At the moment, they were all in the clubhouse for a meeting with the new Titan manager, Warner Olliphant. Press excluded of course, but I knew I'd be able to get a full report after it was over.

Olliphant is a semi-legendary figure. When he played, in the early fifties, he was nicknamed, predictably, Jumbo, but no one has dared call him that to his face for several decades.

He's managed five teams in both leagues in the last dozen years, and never had a losing record. He is one of those little autocrats who can take an undisciplined team and turn it around through sheer force of will. Unfortunately, he is as rigid with the owners and general managers as he is with the players, so he never lasts long with any team.

The Titans were prime candidates for his particular talents. After having made it to the American League playoffs two years ago, they finished a dismal fifth last season, staying out of the basement only because of the unrelenting mediocrity of the Cleveland Indians and New York Yankees.

Ted Ferguson, the Titans' owner, couldn't fire the team, so he took his cue from the boos that greeted the former manager, Red O'Brien, whenever he set foot on the field in the last half of the season, and cut him loose fifteen minutes after the last out of the last game of the season.

He lost the job on merit, but he wasn't the only culprit. His players made the mistake of believing the pre-season scouting reports that said the Titans couldn't miss, and coasted through the first half of the season. By the time they realized that they had to hustle to win the division again, it was too late.

I was glad to see O'Brien go. He was one of those vulgar good old boys who thrive around the game of baseball. The Titan job was his first as manager, but losing it didn't hurt him. Within a month, he had signed on as third-base coach with the Twins, and had enough buddies in the game to keep employed forever. He would manage again.

But not for the Titans. Ferguson had seen enough of O'Brien's loose discipline and hard drinking; and heard enough of his alibis in the three years he was with the team. When he hired Olliphant, the owner announced a new era in Titan baseball; an era in which the outfielders would hit the cut-off man every time, bunts would no longer be popped up, and players would hustle out every ground ball. It was time, he said, not very originally, for good, sound, fundamental baseball. Sometimes I think that baseball people have a special bible of clichés like that.

The pitchers and catchers, who report a week early, had already had a taste of Olliphant's style.

The pitchers, even the stars, were running more laps than they had since the low minors, and the catchers were already black and blue from punishing fielding drills.

My first interview with him hadn't been promising. Olliphant had never dealt with a woman beat writer before, and he made it clear that he didn't like my presence one bit. I just reminded myself that I'd been here for seven years before he arrived, and would probably still be around after he was gone. It was his problem, not mine.

The infielders and outfielders had reported the day before, hence the team meeting, which had been going on for more than an hour. I trusted that my regular informants would be able to give me some juicy stuff.

In the meantime, I couldn't do anything except wait, but it was a pleasant enough chore. Although the sky was grey, the air was warm and fragrant, the grass was brilliant green, and a mockingbird was serenading me with his full repertoire of songs, borrowed from all his feathered pals, from the top of some sort of evergreen beyond the bleachers. It wasn't a bad way to spend a March morning. It sure beat shovelling snow.

The coffee had worked its way through my system, so I decided to head back to the media room for a pee.

Passing the chain-link fence by the box office, I saw that the small sandy parking lot was full and that there were several hundred people lining up for tickets for the Grapefruit League games, which wouldn't start for another week.

The fans had that Florida look. You could tell

the new arrivals by their sunburns, and the permanent residents by their leather skin and horrible taste in clothes – everything that wasn't pastel was either plaid or covered in lurid flowers, and that was on the *men*. Some of them also wore joke baseball caps with phony seagull poop on them.

The women were dressed more sedately, with a few stunning spandex exceptions, and stood slightly bemused, as if wondering at the peculiar transformation retirement had wrought on the staid accountants and dentists they had lived with for all those years. They were surprised by such a late-blooming spousal mid-life crisis.

It suddenly occurred to me that these were my countrymen, and women, but a breed of Canadian I didn't know. Where do they hide out when they're at home? You seldom see seagull-poop caps or hibiscus-print bermuda shorts in downtown Toronto.

I decided that I didn't want to know, turned my back on the miles of varicose veins, and opened the door marked Media Only.

Understanding the connection between happy reporters and favourable reporting, the Titans hadn't scrimped on their complex for the press.

The lounge was the central hangout spot. The white walls were brightened by blown-up action shots of Titans past and present. There were couches and easy chairs, cheerful red carpeting, and a table for playing cards. A bulletin board held clippings, snapshots, and an ever-growing collection of strange headlines and sportswriting clichés. The rest of the reporters and hangers-on were in there, drinking coffee, eating sticky danish pastries, and talking trade rumours.

As I came out of the ladies' room, I heard Bill Sanderson, from the Toronto *World*, trying to defend his latest column, in which he had Joe Kelsey, the left-fielder, headed for the San Francisco Giants.

"It's a natural," he was assuring his dubious audience. "He's gay. San Fran is full of them. Attendance will go up at least a million."

"Sure, Bill," I said. "And what are the Titans going to get back in exchange for the guy who was their MVP last season?"

"I've heard Granyk," he said. "His thirty-seven home runs wouldn't look too shabby here."

"Your theory is a bit flawed," I said. "But what else is new? First of all, Tom Granyk is a first baseman, and last time I looked, the Titans have last year's rookie-of-the-year at first. Second, if they traded Kelsey, they'd need a new left-fielder. The closest they've got in the minors is Domingo Avila, and he's at least a year away.

"The third flaw," I said, counting on my ring finger, "is that Kelsey, despite your inability to deal with his sexual orientation, is the biggest star they've got. The fans would picket the Titan Colosseum if they traded him. And finally, Granyk happens to be forty-one years old and can't score from first on less than a home run. He's washed up."

(Oh, my God. Had I just said someone the age I was yesterday is washed up?)

"That's the talk out west," Sanderson said, smugly. "You'll see."

"I'll put it in the same file as the rest of your rumours," I said. "The circular one."

Sanderson is a bit of a pain in the ass. He's in his mid-thirties, good-looking if you're turned on by

Ralph Lauren ads, and has an ego as big as the players he covers.

He used to be the *World*'s hockey guy until Harold Ballard banned him from Maple Leaf Gardens and he changed beats. Knowing nothing about baseball gave him no humility, even in his first day on the job, and three years later, he is insufferable. Most reporters get their stories by hanging around, listening and watching, talking to players, coaches, and other baseball people, picking up tips, and putting the story together. That's not Sanderson's style.

Partly because the players won't talk to him, his main tool is the telephone, and what he considers a select and reliable network of informants. Most of them are agents and front office people, who use him shamelessly to float stories that will help their clients or teams. Sanderson, in his egotistic enthusiasm, believes he is getting scoops. The rest of us would find him harmless enough, except for two things.

First, every time the *World* prints one of his outrageous stories, our editors immediately order us to match it. This usually involves simply dropping a denial into the last paragraph of our stories, but it's irritating nonetheless. Second, he has convinced his bosses that he is worth about twice the salary I make. That really rankles.

There were half a dozen other media types hanging around the room, listening to Sanderson and waiting for some action. A couple of locals, including the seventy-three-year-old sports editor of the Sunland *Sentinel*, were there for the free coffee.

Keith Jarvis, my other competition, from the tabloid Toronto *Mirror*, had on an outfit that would have looked tasteful standing in the meal line with the winos at the Scott Mission: frayed running shoes, baggy shorts, and a shapeless old tee-shirt that once might have been white. He had a Titan cap over his greasy blond hair, backwards. He was cramming food into his mouth while he read through the major American baseball magazines, cribbing his pre-season analysis. He calls it research.

A couple of photographers were getting their equipment ready, including Bill Spencer from my paper.

"It's ten below at home," he said, smugly. "Snowing."

His daily greeting consisted of a Toronto weather report. I couldn't convince him that I didn't care.

"Got anything lined up?" I asked.

"Medical checkups," he said. "I should be able to get someone looking scared of a needle or something."

"It would be nice if we could get something that hasn't been in the paper every spring for the last decade," I said.

"Find something better, let me know," Spencer shrugged. "I'm just a hired shooter, not an *artiste*."

"Yeah. Fine," I said. I got myself another coffee to wash down the couple of grams of vitamin C I hoped would nuke my cold, and sat in one of the armchairs in the corner of the room.

Lucy was sprawled in the matching chair, one sandal dangling from a foot keeping time to the music on her Walkman, a vacant expression on her face.

Lucy, by the way, is the holder of a legitimate

spring-training press pass as a "reporter" for some two-bit fanzine distributed up and down the Sun Coast. She first showed up about three or four seasons ago. Her journalistic standards and techniques are not exactly the same as mine. The players like her style better, for some strange reason. I guess she's the kind of woman they can understand.

I picked up the St. Petersburg paper to catch up on all the swap meets and bingo games. I'd barely got into it when Hugh Marsh, the Titans' public relations director, came out of his office.

"Warner is ready to meet with the press," he said.

"What is this," asked Sanderson, "a royal command? What if I'm not ready to meet with him?"

"When the Supreme Commander beckons, we obey," said Keith Jarvis, finishing his donut and grabbing his notebook. The rest of us followed him out the door, grumbling. Lucy freshened her lipstick and fluffed her hair.

CHAPTER

2

The sun had broken through the clouds since I went inside, and it was warm enough for me to shed my sweater. The players were out of their meeting, gathered in small groups by the equipment racks outside the clubhouse door. There was a lot of shoving and laughter as they renewed old friendships after the winter. Even if you didn't know which were the new kids – the rookies and minor leaguers – at their first big camp, it was easy to spot them. They were the ones trying to look cool. It was the same every year, but each kid thought he was the only one who felt like wetting his pants.

I was behind Lucy as she wiggled her way toward the manager's office. The reaction was predictable. Rookie jaws dropped, and the veterans leered in a knowing way. Stinger Swain, the third baseman, held his cupped hands in front of his chest and quacked. His buddy Goober Grabowski doubled over laughing. It takes so little to amuse some of these tiny minds.

"Something wrong with your hands, Stinger?" I asked him on the way by. "They're looking awfully crippled. You might not make it past the first cut with hands like those."

He turned them so they were cupped towards my chest.

"Come find out for yourself, honey."

"Don't start, Stinger. We've got a long season to get through," I said, pushing past him.

"Fucking broads," he said, half to himself. "Can't go nowhere in this game anymore without tripping over gash."

I pretended I hadn't heard him. It's easier that way. As I said, it's a long season. I don't have to go looking for aggravation, especially from Stinger Swain. I thought I caught a couple of sympathetic looks from other players as I went through the clubhouse door, but it might have been a trick of the light.

I stopped just inside the locker room and looked around. A clubhouse kid was whistling while setting out lunch on the big work table in the middle of the room: soup, cold cuts, loaves of bread. The players' street clothes were hung in their lockers, fighting for space with golf bags and fishing rods. Joe Kelsey was sitting on the stool in front of his, talking to Tiny Washington, who looked out of place in street clothes. He also looked enormous. He obviously hadn't been worrying about his diet in the first few months of retirement. I went to say hello.

"Is this an interview in progress?" I teased.

Washington had retired at the end of the previous season, after seventeen major-league seasons at first base and one not very productive one as designated hitter. His new job was colour commentary for the Canadian cable sports network. It was going to be interesting to see if the team missed his leadership. He was always good at setting an example, especially for the younger black players.

"Just shootin' the breeze," he rumbled, sticking out his huge hand for me to shake. "Catching up on my man's life."

"You can't do that anymore, Tiny. You're one of us now."

He recoiled in mock horror. Kelsey and I laughed.

"Man, I'm glad you reminded me," Joe said. "I was treating him like a human being. I gotta remember to watch myself from now on."

"Good to see you, Joe," I said, shaking his hand. "Did you winter well?"

"Just fine."

"How's Sandy?"

"Things are still going good," he said.

Sandy Montgomery is Joe's lover, a San Francisco lawyer whose support helped Joe go public with his homosexuality the season before. It was rough the first time around the league, but Joe answered the hecklers in the best way possible. He hit .312 on the season, with 37 home runs, 113 runs batted in, and 42 stolen bases, and would have been the league's most valuable player if the Titans had finished better than they did.

This doesn't mean that he is accepted warmly by his peers. Baseball is a time-warp into the fifties, after all, and the likes of Stinger Swain will never accept him, but enough team-mates jumped the hurdle to make things livable. The fact that they had known and liked him for a long time before he came out made it easier.

Joe, also called Preacher from the days when the born-agains still accepted him as their chapel leader, is one of my favourite players. One outcast appreciates another, for one thing, but that's not all. He had practically saved the life of someone very dear to me the year before. T.C., the eleven-year-old son of Sally Parkes, my best friend and downstairs tenant in Toronto, was next on the hit list of a serial killer the tabloids called The Daylight Stalker.

Joe and Sandy were with me when I realized that the boy was in danger, and the three of us managed to rescue him and hold the killer until the police arrived.

"Catch any crooks lately, Kate?" Tiny was smiling when he asked the question. My freelance detecting is a bit of a joke around the team.

"I've done my best to avoid it," I said.

"Leave that up to Andy," Joe said.

Andy, otherwise known as Staff Sergeant Munro of the Metropolitan Toronto Homicide Squad, is the man I have lived with for almost a year. We met over another murder we were both investigating: his was the cop's angle, mine the reporter's.

"Funny, that's what he says, too," I said. "In this case, I even listen."

"Only in this, I bet," Tiny said.

"He wouldn't know what to do if I agreed with him all the time," I laughed. "Are you coming to the big meeting with the new skipper, Tiny?"

"I have to start sometime, I guess." he said. "Catch you later, Preacher."

We headed towards the manager's office, which had one entrance in the clubhouse, and another outside.

"I don't know what to ask," Tiny said. "I feel like a damn fool."

"That's good. You won't stand out in the crowd," I said. "You know the dumb-assed questions most reporters ask. You've been answering them for eighteen years."

"True enough," Tiny said. "But all anybody ever asked me was what pitch I hit."

"Being a reporter's no different from being a player," I said. "We just have to remember to stay within ourselves and give 110 per cent every day."

We were laughing as we entered the room, and everybody turned and stared at us. Olliphant sat at his desk with his uniform jacket on, arms crossed over his chest. His cap was on the desk in front of him, and even his grey, crew-cut hair bristled with hostility. The body language was unmistakable: "Go away. I don't want you here."

"Sorry," I said. "Are we interrupting something?"

"No, Ms Henry," Olliphant said, emphasizing the dreaded feminist syllable so much that he sounded like a bee. "We were waiting for you to join us."

Since the two available chairs were already occupied, I leaned against the door frame and opened my notebook.

"Maybe you could tell us about your meeting with the players," I said to Olliphant.

"That's confidential," he said, glowering. His

face was lopsided, scarred by the traffic accident that had ended his career. He had been drunk. He also had one glass eye, and I kept forgetting which one to look into when we spoke. The real one wasn't perceptibly more animated.

"Maybe you could just give us the gist of what you talked about," I said.

"We discussed my expectations for the coming season."

"Which are?"

"That we win the World Series," he said.

Interviewing this guy was going to a lot of fun.

"That would be quite a comeback," Sanderson said. "They barely finished fifth in their division last year, and it was a weak division."

"I'm aware of where they finished," Olliphant said. "I also know that they were twenty-three games out of first. I've brought teams back from farther than that."

"You've been in the National League for the last five years," Keith Jarvis reminded him. "Is that going to make your job more difficult?"

"I can read scouting reports," he said. "I have six weeks to get to know my players before the bell rings. I'll know then what this team is really made of."

"What kind of a camp are you going to run?" I asked, as if I didn't know already. "Red's were pretty loosey-goosey."

"So I've heard," Olliphant said, smiling for the first time. I guess it was a smile, anyway. It might have been gas.

"I think it is safe to say that my players will be working a little harder than they are used to," he continued. "Anyone that doesn't care to exert himself will find it expensive."

"Have you fined anyone yet?" Lucy asked.

"That's between me and the players."

Tiny and I exchanged a look. There were going to be a few unhappy campers this spring training.

"In what ways is your camp going to differ from previous Titan camps?" asked Sanderson.

I printed "MORE ATTENTION TO FUNDAMENTALS" on my pad and showed it to Tiny.

"We're going to get right back to basics," Olliphant said. "From what I have seen and heard about this team, we have to pay more attention to good, sound, fundamental baseball."

Tiny stifled a smile.

"I'm talking about fielding, bunting, baserunning, and outfielders hitting the cut-off man. I'm going to take this team back to A-ball until they get it right."

"Don't you think the veterans know how to do those things?" Sanderson ventured.

"If they did, they wouldn't have finished twenty-three games out of first," Olliphant said.

"But still, you must expect some resistance from guys who have been to five or six training camps already," Sanderson persisted, looking for an inflammatory quote. He got it.

"I don't care if a guy's been to twenty camps. If he won't hustle his butt for me, he'll be out of here on it."

"Workouts start tomorrow?" Jarvis asked.

"This afternoon," Olliphant said. "They just got here. Why should they have a day off?"

"What about their physicals?" I asked. "Aren't they scheduled for this afternoon?"

"We're going to do them in shifts. Doc has the schedule. Is that all the questions?"

"Just one more," said Lucy Cartwright, nervously. "Who do you think are the promising rookies?"

The male reporters snickered. Olliphant stared at her coldly for a moment, as if debating whether the question deserved a response. I cringed on her behalf.

"It's too early to tell," he finally said, then got up, put on his cap, picked up his clipboard, and left the room. So much for wide-ranging discussion.

CHAPTER

3

"Guess you're going to have to do your own scouting this spring, Lucy," Sanderson said, snapping his gum in what he apparently thought was an extremely manly way.

"You've got a filthy mind," Lucy said, looking as if she might cry.

"Well, at least it doesn't take penicillin to clean up my *mind*," Sanderson said. As exit lines, it wasn't bad. Lucy was rumoured to have shared a disease with half the Phillies minor-league camp a couple of years back. But it was a cheap shot, and not fair, even to Lucy. I hung back after the rest had gone.

"Are you okay?" I asked her.

"I'm used to it," she said, then went through the outside door quickly. I hesitated. Normally, my definition of sisterly solidarity doesn't include ditzy airheads who make a laughingstock of my profession, but if I didn't support her, there sure as hell wasn't anyone else around the Titan training camp who would. I followed her out the door.

I don't know what I expected to see, but Lucy clearly didn't need my help. She was leaning against the back wall of the clubhouse talking flirtatiously with Glen Milhouse, a rookie catcher, hugging her notebook to her amazing chest like something out of a fifties high-school romance. The girl next door. If you happen to live next door to a bordello.

They were both laughing, and turned, surprised, when I let the door bang behind me. I went around the corner in the opposite direction.

Olliphant hadn't been kidding. While the pitchers lined up to climb into vans to go to the medical centre, the players were all out on one of the practice diamonds, working on fielding. There were three coaches hitting ground balls to the infielders. Another was standing in foul territory in right field with a bazooka, firing towering pop-ups to the outfielders.

I watched for a moment, paying particular attention to Domingo Avila. He was in left field, and the scouting reports were, unfortunately, all too true. I watched him miss two fly balls in a row. The second one, he turned the wrong way, got his feet tangled, and fell down. The ball fell two feet away. He got up, laughing. I hoped Olliphant wasn't watching, for the rookie's sake.

I turned my head at the sound of a commotion by the Titan office and saw that Avila was safe for the time being. Olliphant was yelling at Mary Higgins, the efficient young woman who is in charge of the ground crew.

"When I say the pitcher's mound is unacceptable, your job is to fix it, not to give me lame excuses. I want it done for tomorrow."

"Then you'll have to give me the field back," she said, standing her ground.

"No, lady, you got it wrong again," Olliphant said. "Read my lips. We will be practising until six. Then you can have the field."

"Then I'll have to bring a crew in on overtime tonight and we'll have to use the lights. It's going to be too expensive. If you just give me my field back for half a day, we'll rebuild it without going over budget."

"That's your problem," he said, turned his back, and strode away. She caught me watching and made a rude sign at his retreating back. I shrugged at her in sympathy.

The catchers were halfway to the batting cages under the palm trees, past the left-field grandstand, with Dummy Doran, the bullpen coach. I followed them. Milhouse trotted past me to catch up, looking worried, juggling his bat, glove, shin guards, mask, and chest protector.

He was noticed.

"Kind of you to join us, Rook," Dummy said. "You can go first."

"Thanks, coach," he said. The veterans exchanged grins.

Doran opened the door of the batting cage and bowed like a maître d'hotel for Milhouse to join him. As the kid was passing, Doran took the bat from him.

"You won't be needing this," he said. "Get on your equipment."

"I thought we were hitting," he said.

"Rooks shouldn't think," Doran said. "That's what coaches are for. Now move it!"

He turned and winked at the rest of us, then took up his position next to the pitching machine. Milhouse hustled into the rope mesh and tubular-steel cage, still doing up his chest protector.

"Assume the position!" Doran barked like a drill sergeant. Milhouse hunkered down behind the plate.

Doran held a ball in his hand, poised just above the drive mechanism of the battered blue machine.

"You wearing your cup, Rook?"

Milhouse nodded silently behind his mask and made a surreptitious check with his ungloved hand. Doran fed the ball into the machine, which made a harsh metallic whirring sound before flinging it into the dirt in front of home plate. It bounced off Milhouse's knee.

He scrambled to retrieve it. The other catchers laughed and yelped.

"That was just a change-up," said Doran, holding another ball over the drive tube. "Try a fastball."

I watched for ten minutes. Each pitch took a little bit more arrogance out of the rookie. The other catchers shouted derisive encouragement.

"Suck it up, kid," said Gloves Gardiner, the man whose job Milhouse was after, with a mean laugh.

"Your turn next," Doran said.

Gardiner groaned. I walked over to join him.

"The kid's going to be good," he said, nodding towards Milhouse.

"In Triple A," he added. "I'm not ready to hang 'em up yet."

"I swear to God, you catchers have got to be crazy," I said, watching another fastball bounce off Milhouse's mask. "I bet you still have bruises left over from last season."

"You got to be tough," Gloves said. "That's what they pay me my vast salary for."

Gloves, who makes considerably less than most of the prima donna pitchers he coaxes into their best performances, is one of the few players I have ever encountered with something approaching a sense of irony. He is also one of my best sources on the team.

"What do you make of the new manager?" I asked.

"Might be just the thing this team needs," he said, spitting a brown stream of tobacco just past my right foot. I hate that.

"That's your quote," I said. "Off the record, what went on in the meeting?"

He shrugged.

"Not much. All the usual crap about fundamentals. He spent the winter watching tapes of our games and chewed us out for things we did wrong last June."

"How did the players react?"

"Tried not to laugh, mostly."

"What else?"

Gloves fiddled with the strap of the mask he held in his hand.

"Quote – no matter what we've heard about him, he's as fair as he is tough and that all he asks is that we play hard for him. He won't tolerate goofing off. Unquote. Oh, yeah. Anyone who shows up tomorrow with any hair on his face is fined."

"No beards?"

"No moustaches," he said, stroking his, "no sideburns, no hair except on the head, and that's got to be short."

"I've always wondered if you've got an upper lip," I said.

"Tomorrow's your big chance."

"You'll probably look younger," I teased.

"There's that," he said, brightening. "But I might just look uglier."

"Excuse me, Mr. Gardiner, sir," said Dummy Doran. "When your press conference is over, perhaps you would care to join me for some fundamental exercises."

"See you later," he said, then jogged the few yards to the cage.

"You sure you need me to do this, Dummy? I already did it last year," he said.

"I want to see if you can still crouch on those old knees of yours," was the coach's reply.

I walked over to where Milhouse stood leaning on the cage, sweat streaming down his face, dirt all over his body. He had small beady eyes, a sign of the determination the catcher needs. Or maybe myopia or plain old stupidity.

"That's a pretty good workout," I said. He shrugged.

"We haven't officially met," I said, sticking out my hand. "I'm Kate Henry, from the Toronto *Planet*."

He grunted and shook my hand.

"You're my first woman reporter," he said.

"Is that a problem for you?"

"Women are never a problem for me," he said with a leer that just looked stupid on his baby face.

"It's still early," I said, and walked away.

Just outside the clubhouse, I stopped to introduce myself to Jack Asher, the designated hitter the Titans had picked up as a free agent. He was big and friendly-looking, but so homely he should be playing for the Detroit Tigers. The year before he had been with Olliphant in San Diego.

"Do you anticipate any problems changing leagues?" I asked.

"My big problem isn't with the league, it's with my position. I don't like the DH."

"Guys get used to it," I said. "It's not as if you won a Gold Glove at first base over there."

He looked at me, startled.

"With all respect," I added, straight-faced.

He glared, then laughed.

"As a matter of fact, I was brutal," he said. "Nice to meet a sportswriter who's not a suck. But still, I don't know how to keep my head in the game when I'm sitting on the bench. That worries me."

"A lot of other guys have adjusted to it really well. Not having to worry about fielding really frees up their hitting. Besides, it could add a year or two to your career. As in a year or two more on the payroll."

"That's the kind of talk I like to hear," Asher said.

"You've played for Olliphant before," I said. "Is he as hard-assed as he seems?"

"Yeah," he said. "He is. He's never going to win any popularity contests, but he's good for a team. And, between you and me, from what I've heard, this team could use some of his discipline. And the good news is, he really is fair. If you hustle for him, you'll be out there every day."

"What do reporters have to do?" I wondered, half to myself.

"From what I hear, you take some getting used to," he said. "But they tell me you're fair, too."

"I try to be," I said.

"We'll see," he said. "I'll let you know what I decide."

"I'll be holding my breath."

CHAPTER

4

On my way back to the media room, I was almost totalled in a collision with a waist-high hurricane in jeans and a striped tee-shirt who came hurtling around the corner of the stadium. I grabbed the kid to prevent him from falling and he punched me on the thigh, hard.

"Justin, be nice to the lady," his mother said. She was Tracy Swain, Stinger's wife, carrying a squirming baby in one arm and a diaper bag in the other, but looking as coolly beautiful as ever. She's got that kind of long, straight, shiny, pale blonde hair they use in ads for Swedish tourism.

"I'm sorry about that, Kate," she said. "Sometimes he's a little bit too aggressive. Boys will be boys, you know."

"That's okay," I said. Takes after his dad, I didn't say.

"How's your little girl?" I asked, doing the baby thing.

"Getting into everything," she said. "But adorable."

"What's her name, again?" I had forgotten whether it was Kimberley or some other soap opera name.

"Ashley," she said.

"Right."

I felt a bit awkward. I know and get along with several of the wives, but Tracy was never one of them. Her being married to Stinger pretty much guaranteed that.

"Did you have a nice winter?" I asked.

"It was a winter of great revelation and change," she said. "In December, I welcomed Jesus Christ as my saviour."

"That's nice," I said. What else could I say?

"Now I stand in the brilliant light of God's truth," she said, unself-consciously, as if we were discussing a new diet or workout program.

"What about your husband?" I asked. "Did he experience the same change?"

"Not yet," she smiled brightly, "but I pray for him."

Fat chance of that prayer ever being answered.

"Well, good luck to you," I said.

"Those who have God's grace don't need luck," she said.

"Whatever."

I looked at my watch.

"Oh, no, is that the time? I have to run," I said. "I have a story to write. It's been nice talking to you."

"I'll pray for you, too," Tracy said.

"It can't hurt," I said, picked up my bag, and got out of there.

Before I got to the work room, Millie, the woman in charge of the kitchen and other amenities, called me into the dining room, very pleased, and handed me a florist's box. Inside was a single long-stemmed red rose. No card. I blushed.

"Secret admirer?" Millie asked.

"Not too secret," I said.

"What's the occasion?"

"My birthday."

"I won't ask which one," Millie said, winking conspiratorially. She had a year or two on me.

"I don't care," I said. "I'm forty-two."

"You've got to be kidding," she said.

"I know. I don't look a day over forty-one, right?"

"No, really, honey. You look great."

"Thanks, Millie. But let's not make a big fuss about this. Do you have anything I can use for a vase?"

She rummaged in the cupboard until she found a big ugly green pressed-glass horror, the kind they send from cut-rate florists. The rose looked forlorn in it.

"A bit large, I think," I said. "Have you got a clean beer bottle?"

"That's a shame for such a beautiful flower," she said.

"Just think of it as a metaphor," I said.

"A what?"

"Never mind," I said. Musing about myself as a delicate blossom in crude surroundings, I went into the cubbyhole where my computer was set up. There were a couple of parcels on my work table. One was from my parents in Saskatchewan and the other was from my own address. Sally and T.C. hadn't forgotten either. I decided to open them at home; something to look forward to.

I called my editor, Jake Watson, in Toronto, and promised him a story by 3:00.

"Have you spoken to Spencer about pictures?" I asked.

"Can't say as I have," he answered. "Since you're there, I thought you would take care of it."

"I can barely bring myself to talk to the incompetent son-of-a-bitch," I said. "He thinks it would be a really original idea to shoot pictures of players doing their stretching exercises. Why did they send him?"

"His turn, I guess. They're sure glad to have him out of the office."

"I'd think they would miss him for the weekly shots of lottery winners being given their cheques."

"Now, now, Kate," Jake said. "A photographer is as good as the ideas he is given."

"Since when am I in charge of visuals around here?"

"Since Spencer's turn came up in the rotation. I know you'll get good work out of him."

"Great, Jake. I'm glad you have faith in me. Talk to you later."

"One more thing, Kate."

"Yeah."

"Happy birthday," Jake chuckled. I hung up.

I was starting up my computer, watching random garble march alarmingly across the screen, when hands covered my eyes.

"Guess who, kiddo," the voice said.

There's only one person who calls me that. I grabbed one of the hands and bit it.

"Let's have a bit of respect for your elders," I said, getting up to hug Jeff Glebe, the *Planet's* sports columnist, all six-foot-five of him.

"When did you get in?" I asked, delighted to see him.

"I came right from the airport," he said, grinning all over his slightly goofy face. "I couldn't wait to see you."

"Yeah, sure," I said. "You couldn't wait for free lunch, is more like it."

"That, too."

I looked at my watch. It was 11:30. Morning practice would be winding down soon.

"In an hour, okay? I've got to grab some quotes."

"I'm not writing today."

"Lucky you. You can drink beer and catch up on the gossip."

"Is Juicy Lucy in camp yet?"

"You pig. You're as bad as the rest of them."

"I just like to watch her in action. It's a sociological study."

"Just don't invite her to lunch, if you value our friendship."

"What about breakfast?"

"Not if you value your pecker's health," I said, and went in search of players with facial hair.

The first one I found was Bony Costello, the lugubrious lefthander with the handlebar moustache who heads the starting rotation, just walking in the players' gate.

"Pass your physical?" I asked.

"Well, I've got a few more pounds to lose," he said, gloomily.

"Robins, daffodils, Bony on a diet, all the harbingers of spring," I teased.

"I tried this winter, Kate, honest to god. But my mother keeps feeding me her great pasta. What can I do? I can't offend Mama."

"Maybe she should learn to make salads."

"You don't understand. I'm the thin one in the family."

I looked at his 230-pound bulk and shuddered.

"Look on the bright side, Bony. You'll probably drop five pounds when you shave off your moustache."

He put his hand to his upper lip protectively and looked even sadder.

"That's nothing to joke about," he said. "I don't know if I can pitch without it. I started growing it when I was in a slump my second year in the minors."

Bony, I should point out here, is the most superstitious player I've ever encountered. If he identifies with Samson and believes that his talent comes from a growth of hair under his nose, the Titans' ace could well go down the toilet. I wonder if Olliphant realizes what a neurotic he has heading his starting rotation.

"What I wanted to ask you is whether we can get a picture of you shaving it off."

He looked appalled.

"Kate, there are some things a man has got to do in private."

"Okay, Bony, I understand. Forget it. Tell me what you think of the new manager so far."

We chatted for a few minutes, relatively unproductively. For a truly bizarre guy, Costello is a pretty dull interview. He strains over each answer and brings forth nothing more than inarticulate platitudes. Also, like most pitchers, he is completely self-absorbed. I cut it short when I saw Flakey Patterson, another of the lefthanders, coming out of the clubhouse. Flakey is colourful, good copy and, more to the point, the only Titan with a beard. I asked him about the latest edict.

"Ah, Kate, Kate, count on you to ferret out our little secret," he said. "I'm all for it. Clean body, clean shave, clean mind, pure heart. That's what it takes to win this game."

"You're going to go along with it?"

"Completely. By tomorrow morning, there will not be a region on my body, public or private, that is not as smooth as a newborn child's."

"You've got to be kidding. Legs? Pits?"

"Why would I kid? El Supremo wants clean-shaven, I shall give him clean-shaven."

"Do you plan to do this alone?"

"I have enlisted the assistance of a qualified medical professional, as soon as she is off duty at the clinic. Would you care to be a witness?"

"No thanks," I said, "but I wouldn't mind some photographs of the shaving of the more public bits."

"It would be nice to have a record," he said. "Come to my place at four."

I scribbled down the address, which was a condo complex where a lot of the players stayed, not too far from the apartment hotel in which the *Planet* stashes its writers.

"Is this an exclusive?" I asked, feeling like an idiot. An athlete shaving his head is hardly going to win the National Newspaper Award, but I always like keeping stuff away from the other two papers.

"If you can guarantee me the front page of the sports section and get me a dozen copies," he said.

"That shouldn't be a problem. The Leafs aren't playing."

"The *Mirror* might give me the front page of the whole paper, in colour," he mused.

"And Keith Jarvis called you a has-been last week."

"You have a point," he said. "I appreciate a fine mind like yours. Cruel, but fine. You shall have the scoop."

"I'll see you at four," I said.

"You can wield the blade, if you wish."

"Taking a pass on that one," I said, and left him.

I made the rounds of a few more of the players, picking up predictable quotes. There was general agreement, for the record, that Olliphant's discipline was just what the team needed. The only one who meant it was Atsuo Watanabe, the shortstop, who had had a hard time adjusting to the nonchalance of American players since his arrival from Japan the year before.

I found Spencer and told him where to meet me at 4:00, then went in search of Jeff Glebe. I found him sitting cross-legged on a small patch of grass outside the media room, having a beer.

"First of the day?" I asked. He held up three fingers.

"Come on, big boy, I'd better buy you lunch," I said.

CHAPTER

5

Bill Spencer greeted us as we came in the door.

"Guess you're glad to be down here, eh, Stretch?" he asked Jeff, who hates being called that. "Guess you left a lot of that white stuff behind."

"Yep. There was a whole bunch of winter back there in Toronto," Jeff said.

"Welcome to paradise, buddy. It doesn't get much better than this," Spencer said. We moved on.

"The horrible thing is, he believes it," I said.

We moved into the dining room, which was packed with freeloaders. Millie had laid out the usual spread of cold cuts, cheese, chicken salad, tuna fish, coleslaw, potato salad, and four kinds of bread. There were containers of butter, mayo, and three kinds of mustard; several jars of homemade pickles; and a big hot-pot full of baked beans. It was one of the best free lunches in the Grapefruit League. I spotted a couple of Yankee scouts and the public relations director from the National League office among the usual lineup of reporters and television types.

Jeff and I built ourselves some sandwiches, grabbed a couple of cold beers, and headed outside to sit in the sun. The left-field bleachers served as our picnic table.

"Who's interesting?" Jeff asked me.

"There's a new Dominican," I said. "Domingo Avila. But I have dibs on him for a feature if he looks good."

"I heard about him," Jeff said. "Didn't he go through three levels in the minors last year? He can hit. Power too, if I remember rightly."

"And he's fast. Eighty-seven steals combined last year."

"What's he like?"

"He seems like a nice kid. A real rah-rah guy."

"What's his position?"

"There's the rub, as that great sportswriter Billy Shakespeare once said. He's a natural hitter, but a butcher in the field. He really needs another year in Triple A for seasoning. If he sticks, they would have to use him as the designated hitter, but he's a bit young for that. We'll see how he does here."

"They'd be crazy to rush him."

"Maybe. But the kid can hit and the fans are hungry for new faces. It will all depend on Olliphant."

"Still, he's a good story."

"For me," I reminded Jeff. "My beat. Columnists defer."

"Yes ma'am. What else?"

"It's still early days. But I know one thing. These

guys are going to have to do more than go through the motions for a change."

"Olliphant's tough?"

"Like the Pope's right-wing."

"It will look good on them."

"The golf courses and dog tracks may have to declare a day of mourning, though."

Jeff finished off the last bite of his third sandwich and looked with dismay at his empty plate.

"You think there's any dessert?" he asked.

"Oh, God, how do you stay so thin?"

"Come on, let's go check. Maybe Millie made pie."

"I'll pass, thanks. Bring me back a coffee."

"Come with me. Just see if there's pie. You can't live on that one little sandwich."

"I've never met anyone so obsessed with his stomach," I said, getting up and gathering my garbage together. "I'll leave you to the pie. I have a story to write. I've got to be somewhere at four."

"Want to have dinner later?"

"Maybe," I said.

We walked back to the media centre. Jeff held the door for me. Then I understood why he insisted upon my joining him. There wasn't any pie. Just cake, with one great big candle burning in it, and a bunch of idiots singing "Happy Birthday." I hate this kind of thing, but Jeff was behind me, blocking the door. And singing. Off key. I could feel myself blushing. Or maybe it was a hot flash, given my age.

"Thanks, guys," I said, when the applause was over. "You really know how to humiliate a person."

I cut the cake, then Hugh Marsh called for silence.

"Kate, we have a small token of our esteem for

you. We're all part of the same family, and we think this little gift is emblematic of your place in that family."

I accepted the wrapped package warily. The way they were watching me, I knew it had to be a joke. It was. Inside the box was a jockstrap, dyed pink, with ruffles on the pouch. Somebody must have made his wife sew them on.

"Gee, guys, that's really sweet. How did you know my size?"

The celebration ended quickly enough. I had a token piece of cake, which was homemade, and delicious, covered in gooey fudge icing. Lucy Cartwright approached me just as I was licking it off my fingers.

"Happy birthday, Kate!" she twinkled. "I can't believe you're really forty-two. Like that's really incredible, you know? I mean, you're older than my mom, but you don't look it."

"Thanks, Lucy," I muttered. "You're too kind."

"No, really, I'm not kidding you," she said. "You know if you changed your hair a bit and didn't dress quite so straight? You know? I mean, you could look like you were like thirty. Maybe we could go shopping sometime."

Oh, great, just what I needed. A makeover session with Teen Tart of Greater Tampa Bay. We could get matching crotch-notching pedal pushers? And spike heels? And she could teach me to talk all the time in question marks?

"It's not a good time right now," I said. "I'm not really much of a shopper."

"Yeah, I could tell," she said. "And we could do a trade, you know? Like maybe you could give me some tips on sportswriting?"

She stood, smiling eagerly, flirting. It was the only way she knew to interact.

"What are you working on now?" I asked.

"Well, like I told Mr. Olliphant, I really want to do something on the rookies, you know? Some of them have played here, and some of them will be playing here this year. That's what interests my readers."

Her readers? Good grief!

"I guess you know as much as I do," I shrugged. "I saw you talking with Milhouse. He's a possibility. So's Avila."

"Yes, I know Domingo," she said. "We, like, dated when he was playing here at the beginning of last season? I taught him most of the English he knows, but it's still not very good, you know? My Spanish is better."

"Better than mine, I'm sure. I speak a bit, but not enough for a real interview."

"Well, if you want me to help, I will," she said.

"That's very kind, Lucy. I would appreciate that."

"Okey-dokey," she said. "I've got to go now. Happy birthday again."

She wriggled across the room, picked up her notebook and went out the door.

I was still shaking my head when I sat down at my computer.

CHAPTER

6

The story I filed wasn't going to win any awards, but I got it done and in by the time I was due to go to Flakey's.

I got into the stupid little generic tin can I had rented for the duration, thinking longingly of the quirky Citroën Deux Chevaux sitting at home in my garage, gathering dust. The rental, with its automatic transmission, was no fun at all to drive.

I turned out of the parking lot onto the side street down towards the beach, past block after block of almost identical bungalows, each with a large car in the driveway and a tidy lawn. The houses, which had no character and little charm, looked as if they had all been built in the past twenty years, designed by a cookie-cutter. The gardens were tight and contained, rigid despite the kind of climate that could create riotous vegetation. And there were no people, no kids playing, no retirees working in the garden, no signs of life at all. This part of Florida always reminds me of one of those science-fiction movies where alien beings have spirited away entire populations.

Flakey's condo was in a two-storey stucco building painted in that peculiar pale puce that is so popular down here, with rustic shingling on the roof. It was a beach-front complex built around a pool. This is another strange Floridian phenomenon. Why anyone would rather swim in a chlorine-tainted concrete box in the ground than in God's blue ocean is beyond me, but poolside was packed when I arrived just before 4:00.

Players' wives sunbathed or sat around one of the round patio tables playing cards, while they kept an eye on the kids paddling in the shallow end. I could tell they were players' wives by the diamonds strewn around their bodily parts.

There were no players around. They get enough sun on the job. My sister-in-sportswriting, Lucy Cartwright, was perched on a deck chair, talking with Glen Milhouse and Domingo Avila, who were having a hard time concentrating on their answers. She had taken off her shirt, and her tube-top had them mesmerized.

A guy wearing coveralls was vacuuming the hot tub and looking as though he was in charge. I asked him where I'd find Flakey.

"He expecting you?" he asked, suspiciously.

"I have an appointment at four," I said.

He grunted, then pointed up the stairs at the corner of one of the side wings.

"Up there, first door," he said. I thanked him and climbed the stairs. He watched me all the way.

Flakey answered my knock almost immediately, dressed in jeans and a short dressing gown that looked like silk, and probably was. Black, with embroidered dragons.

"Your photographer's been here for half an hour," he said, looking grim. I didn't blame him.

"That's strange," I smiled. "I told him four o'clock."

"I was in the neighbourhood anyway," Bill Spencer said, getting slowly up from his chair. His shirttail was half-out and he had a can of beer in his hand. "I thought I'd get things set up and ready to go."

He had used up all sorts of equipment around the room. There were lights bouncing off the walls and ceiling, and one of those weird umbrellas photographers use. His camera was on a tripod, set up a few feet away from a stool centred against a blank wall painted a light chartreuse. Does Florida get a special deal on paint factory mistakes?

"Ah, it's your well-known Yousuf Karsh imitation, I see. I thought we'd just get some candid snaps," I said.

"I didn't want to take any chances," he said.

Flakey came back into the room carrying a couple of cans of cold beer and handed me one. He was followed by a smiling oriental woman in a nurse's uniform.

"This here is May," Flakey said. "She's going to shave me."

"Okay, let's do it," I said.

Flakey sat on the stool and pulled funny faces while May clipped his hair and beard short. Then she covered his head and face with shaving foam from a can and got to work with the first of several disposable razors.

The result was startling. By the time she got to his eyebrows, even Bill Spencer was giggling.

"You look like an egg," I said.

"No, he looks like an extraterrestrial," May said. "A man from Mars."

"I think it gives me a certain dignity," said Flakey, trying to look it. He didn't succeed.

We took a few more shots of May shaving his legs, then I told Bill to pack up his gear.

"I think perhaps we'll leave before this begins to get X-rated," I said. Spencer looked disappointed.

"If you like, I could stick around," he said to Flakey, hopefully. "Maybe you'd like some souvenirs."

"Yeah, that would be great," Flakey said. "I've got to get a full frontal shot for my scrapbook."

"I'll leave you to it," I said. "I've got to go."

"What's wrong, Kate?" Flakey asked. "You afraid of seeing my dick? You see it every day in the clubhouse."

"That's out of duty, not choice," I said. "This time I choose to leave. I'll see you tomorrow."

As I let myself out the door, Patterson was unzipping his pants.

Cat-calls greeted me as I came down the stairs towards the pool. Stinger Swain was lying on a plastic lounge chair, next to a cooler full of beer.

"Now we know why you give Flakey such good ink," he yelled. "He's giving you a little on the side."

This rapier-like wit was greeted by guffaws from his buddy Goober Grabowski.

"Get your mind out of your pants," I said. It was the best I could come up with on short notice.

"Leave her alone, Stinger," said Gloves Gardiner, from the other side of the pool. Looking around, I realized that most of the team was there, with their families. They had set up a couple of barbecues.

"What's going on, guys?" I asked. "A little pre-training party?"

"Yeah, and you're not invited," shouted Grabowski.

"Well, I'm just going to cry all the way home, then," I said.

Gloves came over, wearing an apron with clever barbecue jokes on it. His wife, Karin, was with him. We exchanged greetings.

"Sorry about this, Kate," Gloves said. "Team party. No press."

"Hey, I don't mind. I didn't come here for a party. I'm working. No problem."

As I drove off, I realized that I had been protesting too much to Gloves. It wasn't that I wanted to stick around the players' party, but my exclusion reminded me of my own lack of social life and made me lonely. Especially on my birthday. It's times like this that I hate my job.

I was working myself up to some fine self-pity. That wasn't how I wanted to spend my birthday, either. I cut into a mall parking lot and stopped at the liquor store. A half-bottle of champagne wouldn't break the budget. If I was going to feel sorry for myself, I might as well do it in style.

I also bought myself some flowers to go with Andy's rose, and was feeling quite cheery when I arrived back at my efficiency apartment. I put the champagne in the mini-fridge to chill, while I showered and changed into jeans and an old police department sweatshirt of Andy's that I wear when I miss him. Then I did a fast tidy so I would deserve the champagne.

By the time the wine was cold, the newspapers had been stacked in a corner, my clothes were all put away, and the flowers on the coffee table made the impersonal place quite homey. I took the bottle, a glass, the flowers, and my presents out to the tiny grimy balcony, ready to toast the sunset. I could just see it if I leaned way out and looked to the left.

I had just popped the cork when I heard a knock at the door. It was Jeff Glebe, with a bottle of champagne in one hand and a plastic bag in the other.

"I couldn't let you celebrate your birthday alone," he said, handing me his offerings. "I'm sorry they're not wrapped."

"You shouldn't have," I said, genuinely touched. "Come in. You've saved me from the sin of solitary pleasure."

He looked alarmed.

"Drinking alone," I said.

I put his champagne in the fridge – it was Californian, mine was French – and fetched another glass. We toasted me and the sunset, then I opened his present.

It was a book, a new novel by a woman writer I had heard of but not read. It was thoughtful of Jeff. One reason we get along is because we both like to read things other than box scores. It sets us apart from many of our colleagues.

"Thanks, Jeff," I said. "You're a real friend. This wouldn't be about the perils of middle age, would it?"

"No way," he said, raising his right hand in a boy

scout salute. "I checked it out myself. It's about getting older is getting better."

"Thanks, pal," I said. I got up and kissed him. There was an awkward silence. I broke it.

"We might as well make it a real party," I said. "You can watch me unwrap my other presents."

The parcel from Saskatchewan was also a book. My parents were obviously trying to improve my mind and keep me on the political straight and narrow: it was a collection of reminiscences about T.C. Douglas, the former premier of the province and federal New Democratic Party leader, a Henry family hero. I was delighted.

There were two gift-wrapped packages in the parcel from home. Sally and T.C. (Douglas is a hero in their household, too) had each sent a gift. T.C.'s was another book.

"This is getting monotonous," I laughed, holding the package up to show Jeff. "I'm opening Sally's first."

I should have been warned by the card, which read, "For a woman in her prime and on the loose." Inside the innocuous-looking box was a low-cut, backless nightie in a leopard-skin print, edged with black lace. When I pulled it out, a box of condoms fell on the floor. Leopard-print condoms.

I laughed as hard at Jeff's blushing face as at the scandalous gift.

"There are some who don't think I'm washed up at forty-two," I said. Jeff is barely into his thirties.

I repacked the box and opened T.C.'s package. It made me laugh, too. It was called *Be Your Own Private Eye: An Amateur's Guide to Detection.*

"Just what I really need," I laughed, holding the book up so Jeff could see the title.

"Oh, God," he said. "There'll be no stopping you."

"And now, my fine young friend, I'm going to change into something presentable and you can take me out for a splashy dinner."

"Will Denny's do?"

"Not on your life," I said.

CHAPTER

7

Three hours later, and a bottle of wine more relaxed, Jeff and I sat in a booth made from wagon wheels in The El Rancho Roadhouse, watching bank tellers and time-share salesmen in cowboy hats doing the two-step around a giant dance floor. In front of us on the table (which had seashells imbedded in it from the joint's previous incarnation as a seafood restaurant), were long-neck Lone Star beers with side shots of tequila.

We'd had a quiet dinner in the only decent restaurant in town, a small French place that serves good duck and lacks the three curses of Florida tourism: Happy Hour, Early Bird Specials, and the salad bar. It was my idea to try out The El Rancho, an ersatz cowboy bar a ten-minute walk from the apartment hotel we both called home. Or a fifteen-minute stagger if things got out of hand.

I was feeling very mellow, watching the ripe

young women and muscular young men posing at the long bar, as if they were auditioning for some beer commercial. Looking ever so cool but crying out through their body language: "Choose me! *Please* choose me!"

"Cheer up, Kate," said Jeff. I looked at him, surprised.

"I'm extremely cheerful," I said. "You will find as you mature that it is possible to be philosophical without being depressed."

"Huh," he said.

"Huh, what?"

"I never noticed before that you sound like my mother when you drink," he said.

"Oh, piss off," I said.

"That's better. What are you thinking about?"

"I'm thinking about what it was like to be in my twenties," I said, nodding towards the bar. "I'm thinking about all the things these kids don't know. I'm thinking about how the things that scare them now don't look so bad twenty years down the road."

"Like what?"

"Like going home alone. Like not being as pretty or as handsome as your best friend. Like getting old."

"This is cheerful?" Jeff said. "Sounds to me like singing the birthday blues. Come on. You're not old."

"I'm forty-two, Jeff. To these kids, that's way past it. You should see the way the women look at me in the ladies' room. They stop talking when I come in. And the men, their eyes slide past me as if I wasn't there. And you know what? It's not so horrible. I've got so much more than they have, in experience, in confidence, in money, status, everything, but they pity me because I have wrinkles. It would be funny if it wasn't so sad."

I drained my tequila and signalled to the waitress for another round.

"See that girl at the end of the bar?" I asked. I motioned to a dark, shy, awkward young woman, five inches taller than her two bouncy friends, Lucy Cartwright clones. They all looked to be in their late teens, early twenties.

"She's having a terrible time. She's lonely. No one has asked her to dance. She doesn't have the moves. The guys are all over her two friends. Right now she's cursing herself for agreeing to come tonight. She's trying to figure out how to get home, to disappear with some dignity."

"Come on, Kate. Ditch the melodrama."

"No, no," I said. "I'm right. I know. I've been there myself, and it was agony. I wish I could just talk to her. I would tell her all sorts of stuff she'll know one day. Like that cute doesn't last. That when she and her friends are thirty, she's going to be the beautiful one. That those guys the airheads are attracting are all jerks anyway. That I would bet on her over anyone else in the room."

I lit another cigarette.

"I could tell her that and save her a lot of grief," I went on. "But she wouldn't believe me. She'd just think I was some pathetic middle-aged woman who's had too much to drink. That's the really crazy truth about the whole deal."

I felt tears in my eyes. Not for me. Not for middle-aged me, but for her, and for the me who used to be her. Jeff was looking down at the table, fiddling with my lighter, avoiding my eyes. I laughed, and wiped the tears away with the back of my hand.

"Come on, young fellow. Aren't you going to ask the old broad to dance?"

"I'm not sure I can stand the damage to my reputation," Jeff sighed, getting up from the table. "Those young beauties won't give me a look once they see me with you."

"You lost your chance when you turned thirty, Bubbah," I said, taking his hand. "I sure enough do hope you know how to two-step."

I had learned the dance one wild off-night at Billy-Bob's in Fort Worth when the Titans and Rangers were rained out. Jeff did his best to follow me, but we weren't Fred and Ginger. If I'd been writing the movie, the young whipper-snappers would have formed a clapping circle around the two of us as we dazzled them with our grace and sex appeal, but, as it turned out, I was glad when the song ended and we could escape the dance floor spotlights and stumble back to our table. Maybe that last tequila hadn't been such a hot idea.

"Maybe that last tequila wasn't such a hot idea," I said.

"Hey, lighten up," Jeff said. "If we can't get a little drunk on your birthday, what's the point?"

His logic made such sense to us both that we ordered another round.

They kicked us out when the bar closed at 2:00, arms around each other, partly in companionship and partly to help us stay upright. The moon was full over the water.

"Beach walk!" Jeff said, steering us in the general direction. "Moonlight beach walk!"

We both took off our shoes and walked by the edge of the water. I'm afraid we sang, too. "José Cuervo (You Are a Friend of Mine)" and "Older Women Make Beautiful Lovers," in bad harmony. It was quite chilly. My miserable cold had been helped by the medicinal spirits with which I'd been dosing myself, but sloshing through ankle-deep ocean set me sneezing again. I couldn't stop. I put together a string of about fifteen, which, for some reason, we found hysterically funny.

We sat on the sand to catch our breath. Jeff suddenly turned serious.

"Are you really depressed about your birthday?" he asked. "You shouldn't be. You don't seem older. You don't look it. You don't act it."

"Thanks, Jeff," I said. "You're a pal."

He didn't understand, of course. It wasn't that I wanted people to think I was younger than forty-two. I wanted people to think that forty-two is just a perfect age to be.

"No, really," he said, with earnest, drunken intensity. "I think you're great."

He was crouched in front of me, his hands on my shoulders, looking into my face in the moonlight. Neither of us spoke. Somewhere, a car backfired. He kissed me.

I wish I could say that I gracefully detached myself with a gentle rebuke, reminding him of his wife, and my whatever, at home, but I didn't. We got into some pretty passionate necking. Only the cold kept us from going any further.

"Let's go home," Jeff said, finally. He got up and took my hand, helping me up. We walked along the beach in charged silence, still holding hands.

We passed by a thatched cabana that served as a beach bar behind one of the big hotels, with deck chairs chained to a post in a row next to it. There was someone sprawled on one of the chairs in the shadows, covered with a dark beach towel. A beer can lay on the sand, partly under the chair.

"Looks like someone else has been doing some celebrating," Jeff said.

"It's cold. Do you think we should wake him up?"

"Nah, let him sleep it off," Jeff said.

"We can't," I said, pulling him across the sand.

"Kate, this is Florida. You don't want to get involved."

"Come on," I argued. "We can handle some drunk. No one should sleep outside. It's probably a hotel guest."

"All right, do your good deed," he said.

We were a few feet away from the chair.

"Excuse me?" I said. "Hello! In the chair! Maybe you'd better sleep somewhere else."

That didn't work.

I approached the chair, reached out, and touched the person on the shoulder. Jeff came up behind me.

"It's a woman," he said.

Blonde curls were showing above the top of the towel. I pulled it off.

"Oh, my God," I said, turning away.

It was Lucy Cartwright lying there, and I could tell from the amount of blood that she wasn't ever going to wake up.

CHAPTER

8

I had covered my face with my hands, but when I looked out, the horrible sight hadn't gone away. Lucy's face was unmarked, and she looked startled, with her eyes wide open. Her chest was just a pulpy mess, the blood black in the moonlight. I couldn't look away. I was suddenly very cold. Jeff was down the beach, vomiting under a palm tree.

"We've got to call the police," I said, when he got back.

"You go to the hotel and call," Jeff said. "I'll stay here."

"I'm not going anywhere alone," I said. "And I'm not going to leave you alone, either. The murderer might still be around. It's too late for her."

"You're right," he said.

We walked quickly across the sand and past the pool to the back door of the hotel. I felt dizzy, and kept fighting the impulse to look back. The front desk was beyond the elevators. The clerk on duty was reading in the office behind the desk. I rang a bell to get his attention. He was young and earnest-looking, and looked irritated at the interruption. He kept his place in his book with his finger. The Bible. It figured.

"Please call the police," I said. "There's a dead body on the beach. I think she's been murdered."

"Oh my gosh," he said. He went to the switchboard and dialled a number, then pointed to the phone at the end of the reception desk. I picked it up.

"Sunland Police Department."

"I'm calling from the Gulf Vistas Hotel," I said, not very calmly. "I've just found a dead person on the beach."

Sounding slightly bored, as if corpses were always popping up in Sunland, the officer asked for my name and details of the body. When he realized it wasn't another senior citizen with a heart attack, he got a little more interested.

"Stay right there," he said. "We'll have someone with you within five minutes."

I hung up.

"What's your name?" I asked the clerk.

"Barry," he said.

"Well, Barry. Do you think there's a chance we could get a cup of coffee?"

"The kitchen's not open," he said.

"I didn't ask if the kitchen was open, I asked if I could get a cup of coffee," I snapped. "Surely you've got a pot back there somewhere."

"I don't drink coffee," he said, smugly. "It's bad for you."

What an asshole.

"Look, kid, we're going to have to be hanging around here for a while," I said. "We are also going to have a bunch of cops here in a matter of minutes and you know they're going to want coffee, so I suggest you might rustle some up."

"We'll mind the desk," Jeff added.

Barry left in a huff, taking his Bible with him.

"You're a tiger," Jeff said.

"He's a jerk," I answered.

I went and sat in one of the pink lobby chairs, under the lithograph of flamingos and palm trees. Jeff took the other one, under the lithograph of sandpipers in the sunset. I handed him a mint I'd taken out of a bowl at the desk, and we both stared at the door, as if waiting for a performance to begin.

"There's one thing about finding a body," I said. "It sobers you up right quick."

I could hear the sirens coming. Two cop cars pulled up outside the entrance, and four cops came running in, hands on their guns.

"Relax, guys," I said, standing up. "The body's already cold."

One of them, older than the rest, with some authority to him, walked over.

"Officer Sweeney," he said. "Are you the lady who called?"

I introduced myself and Jeff.

"She's out back by the beach bar," I said. "We know her. She's Lucy Cartwright."

Sweeney's reaction was no reaction at all. His face tightened, just perceptibly, and one of the other officers, young and blond, looked quickly at him, then away.

"We're sportswriters from Toronto," I explained,

filling the silence. "That's how we know her. She comes out to Horkins Field."

"Will you show us where please, Miss?" Sweeney said. We headed towards the back door. "Or maybe you'd rather stay inside and let Mr. Glebe do it."

"I can handle it," I snapped.

I looked at Jeff.

"But if you would like to stay here, that's fine with me."

He glared.

"We'll both go," he said.

The six of us walked past the pool and down to the beach in awkward silence. I stopped when we came in sight of the bar. I pointed.

"She's over there," I said.

"You just wait right here," Sweeney said. "We're going to need to talk to you afterwards."

My legs felt a bit wobbly. I sat down on the concrete wall separating the pool from the beach, shivering. Jeff joined me, and put his arm around me.

"Thanks," I said.

We were there for a long time, just watching.

There was lots of action, fast. First, one of the cops pulled the cruiser to the edge of the parking lot and left it running, with its headlights illuminating the grisly scene. I laughed when the phrase caught my mind, because it was such a newspaper cliché. I reminded myself not to use it in print.

Sweeney, overseeing the scene, took stakes and rolls of yellow crime-scene tape out of the trunk, and he and the two others put up a fence all around the area.

More cops arrived, gradually. First, more uniforms. Then a couple of guys wearing sweats, who looked as if they had been dragged out of bed. One of them was slightly older than the other and seemed to be in charge. I thought about Andy, and the nights he had been called away from our warm bed to scenes just like this, and felt a surge of sympathy for them. It's a hell of a way to make a living.

A generator truck parked on the beach and fired up noisily. Soon the scene was illuminated by half a dozen floodlights. It would have been festive, if it hadn't been so gruesome.

Half an hour passed, and I had just about decided that they had forgotten about us, when one of the uniformed officers pointed us out to the guy in charge. He called over the other man in sweats and sent him jogging across the sand to us.

He was, inevitably, blond and fit-looking, with a no-nonsense tightness to his sharp features and an almost military bearing, despite the casual clothes. His sweatsuit was navy blue, with red and white trim. Of course.

"You're the ones who found the body?" he asked. We nodded. "We're going to be a while. You'll be more comfortable waiting in the lobby. There's coffee."

"Why can't we leave?" I asked, getting to my feet. My knees creaked, another birthday reminder. "We'll let you know where to find us."

"Detective Sergeant Barwell will need to talk to you," he said. "He's the commander of the case squad."

"Who are all those people?" I asked.

"Just investigators, ma'am."

"There are so many of them."

"Some are from the Sunland Police Department. Some are crime technicians from the county sheriff's office. The lady is Doc Wilson. She's the medical examiner. She's got a crew with her. Then there's the state attorney. He's the guy in the suit."

"And who are you?"

"Detective Sargent," he said.

"I thought the detective sergeant was the other guy."

'No, ma'am, sorry. Sargent's my name. Jim Sargent. S-a-r-g-e-n-t."

"So when you get promoted, you'll be Detective Sergeant Sargent?'

"Yes ma'am."

I giggled. He didn't.

"Sorry," I said.

"You're not the first," he said, wearily.

"I'm sure."

"Let's go inside, Kate," Jeff said. "I'm freezing."

"I'll come with you," Sargent said. "I have a couple of questions."

There was a shout down on the beach. One of the uniforms had found something, by a palm tree. Sargent watched with interest. I recognized the tree. So did Jeff.

"Excuse me, detective," he said. "I guess I'd better tell you something."

He explained his responsibility for the mess under that particular palm. Sargent, straight-faced, thanked him.

"I'll just go get that straightened out," he said. "I'll catch up with you inside."

CHAPTER

9

It was warmer inside, and there was a coffee urn set up on a table next to the entrance to the bar. Barry had given up on scripture for the night, and was sitting at the desk, all ears – to no avail at that particular moment, because the four men standing around fell silent when we came into the lobby. They were dressed in jeans, plaid shirts, and down vests, and were either plainclothes cops or alligator hunters getting an early start on the day. Very macho. They watched suspiciously as we filled styrofoam cups and did the sugar and cream thing. We took our coffee back to the chairs under the sandpipers and waited.

The phone rang. Barry picked it up, then motioned to one of the men, who picked up the house phone.

"Where the fuck are you?" he asked. Barry cringed and glanced my way, perhaps concerned about the sullying of my lady-like ears. "Well, I'm sorry about that, but you better get your ass over to the Gulf Vistas, pronto. We got a cold one."

He listened for a moment, then laughed.

"Well, that's just tough, buddy. The dragon lady needs her splatter guy. . . . Okay, buddy. See you in five. . . . All right. Ten. Sure that's all you need?"

He laughed again, then hung up.

"Says he's just about done," he explained to his buddies.

"Speedy Gonzales strikes again," said one of the guys.

"Wonder who the chick is," said another.

"Guy probably does, too," said the third. Guffaws all around.

"Better get back to work," said the one who had talked on the phone.

There was grumbling agreement, and they drained their cups and left them sitting on the counter. The smoker in the group took a couple of greedy last drags on his cigarette before stubbing it out and following the rest out the door. Barry went back to his Bible.

"What do you think a splatter guy is?" I asked.

"I don't think I want to know," Jeff said, then got up and began to pace the lobby.

"Quit with the tiger imitation," I said. "You're making me dizzy."

"I just want to get out of here," he said. "How long are they going to keep us?"

"Longer than we want, that's for sure. Don't sweat it. It will just make it worse."

Jeff paced back, and threw his lanky frame into the backbreaking soft chair. I lit another cigarette.

"I wish I smoked," he said.

"Passes the time," I agreed, then coughed.

"Passes it right into an early grave."

"There's that, too."

The lobby door opened, and we looked up, expecting some official police presence. Instead, we heard singing, in a deep baritone which made up in volume for what it lacked in tune.

"I could have daaaaanced all night . . ."

The sound was followed quickly by a small, portly gentleman clad in what some call "full Cleveland," his white shoes and matching belt setting off plaid trousers, a striped shirt, and a patterned bow tie. The man's hair was white, but he had a lusty sparkle in his eye and a heartbreaker's smile as he waltzed his companion through the lobby. She, thickened in the middle, with freshly permed hair and an embarrassed but loving look on her face, was wearing a powder-blue shirtwaist dress in some sort of silky synthetic.

"*Jerry*, there are people watching," she said.

He stopped in mid-twirl, looked over his shoulder at us, and winked.

"More night-owls," he said. "What's the matter, locked out of your room?"

"That's none of our business, honey," his wife said, then turned to us. "Please forgive my husband. We've been to a celebration."

"That's right," he said. "It's not every day my first grandson gets married. Wouldn't you say that was a reason to kick up my heels?"

"The best," I said.

"We've just come from the rehearsal dinner," his wife explained. "At the country club. It was a barbecue."

"Steaks this thick," he said, measuring two inches between his thumb and forefinger. "Martinis. Wine. Dancing. They sure know how to entertain down here. Where are you folks from?"

"Canada," Jeff said.

"Toronto, I bet. The Titans train here," he said. We allowed that he was right on the money. "We sure hate them where we come from. Almost as much as the Yankees."

"Where's that?" Jeff asked.

"Akron, Ohio," he said. Close. "We're Indians fans. And the Reds, in the other league. We're the Johnsons, Jerry and Judy. Pleased to make your acquaintance."

We began to introduce ourselves, but were interrupted by the arrival of Detective Sargent.

"Excuse me folks," he said, politely. "We have some police business here."

"Well, that's fine," Jerry said, quickly. "It's about time I took my beautiful bride off to bed. Come on, sugar-pie."

As the elevator doors closed, I heard her voice, saying "They don't look like criminals, do they, honey-bun?"

Sargent grunted at us and went to pour himself a coffee.

"Sorry to keep you waiting," he said, coming back across the lobby and sitting down. "That's what this business is about. Hurry up and wait."

"Hey, we had nothing better to do," said Jeff. "Except maybe sleep."

"Makes two of us," Sargent said. "Three of us."

"Can I ask you a question first?" I asked.

Sargent grunted again.

"Some of your men were talking about a splatter guy. What's that?"

Sargent almost smiled.

"That's what Doc Wilson calls Guy Charon," he said, pronouncing the name nothing like its obvious French-Canadian roots. "He's one of her crime-scene investigators. Specializes in blood stains."

"I knew I didn't want to know," Jeff said.

"There are some really interesting patterns out there," Sargent said, obviously wishing he didn't have to babysit witnesses.

Jeff shut his eyes.

"I forgot. Your friend's a bit squeamish," he said, not bothering to disguise his contempt.

"It's hardly surprising," I said, wanting to defend Jeff. It felt like his manhood was under attack, and he was in no condition to defend himself.

"Takes some people that way," Sargent said.

"Ours is not a line of work where we see a lot of gore," I explained.

"Didn't seem to bother you any."

Was that an insult?

"Can I break up this meeting of the cast-iron stomach society?" Jeff asked. "I'd like to get home to bed."

"Me, too," I said.

"That makes three of us, again," Sargent said. "But I got a job to do."

He pulled a notepad out of his jacket pocket.

"Names?"

We told him.

"Address?"

I gave him the name of our hotel, and our room numbers.

"You're not together?"

"No," Jeff said. "We work together."

"You were working at two-thirty in the morning?"

"I can't see that it's any of your business," I said.

"Okay, it's like that," Sargent said.

"No it's not," we said, overlapping each other.

"Not what?" Sargent asked. Jeff began to laugh. So did I.

"What's funny?" Sargent asked, suspiciously.

"Nothing's funny," I said. "My sense of humour just kicked in."

"About time, too," Jeff said.

The tension broken, Jeff and I got on with the job of describing everything we had seen when we found Lucy on the beach. It didn't take long. Sargent got up and put his notebook back in his pocket. We got up, too.

"So we can go?"

"Not until you talk to Detective Sergeant Barwell."

"And that will be when?" I asked.

Sargent shrugged.

"When he's through outside."

"Finished with the splatters," Jeff said.

"You got it," Sargent said, looking almost cheerful.

After he left, I went to get another coffee, and almost bumped into a good-looking guy wearing jeans, cowboy shirt, and ostrich-skin boots. We'd last seen him at The El Rancho, slightly less rumpled. I thought he was another hotel guest, until he asked for Dr. Wilson.

"Are you the splatter guy?" I asked. I couldn't resist.

"Yeah," he said. "Who are you?"

"Witness," I said. "She's out back."

"Thanks," he said, looking confused. "Haven't I seen you before somewhere?"

"Could be, cowboy," I said, and sashayed back to my seat.

"Cute," Jeff said.

"This sitting around is getting me punchy," I explained.

"It's pissing me right off."

"Right. I feel like we're suspects, not witnesses."

"Look who's talking," Jeff said. "The cop-lover."

"That's a specific, not a generic, attraction," I explained, yawning. "Oh, God. I wish I'd brought a book."

"Maybe Barry will lend you his Bible."

"Another ten minutes and I might ask for it."

I was saved from sanctity by the arrival of the second sweatsuit.

"I'm Detective Sergeant Troy Barwell," he said, crossing the room. "Sorry to keep you waiting."

"No sorrier than we are," Jeff said.

"We'll do anything we can to help," I added, sending Jeff a look. Why antagonize the guy?

He looked to be about thirty-five, muscular under a layer of fat, like an athlete past his prime. He was wearing an old grey sweatsuit that looked worn and comfortable, and he was good-looking, in a beady-eyed sort of way.

"I've seen what you had to say to Detective Sargent," he said. "I just have a few more questions."

"Go ahead," I said.

"Did you see or hear anyone else as you walked down the beach? Anyone at all?"

"No," we both said.

"You're sure," he said.

I shrugged.

"Why would I lie? Yes, I'm sure."

"You left the bar at two a.m., is that right?"

"Whenever they closed."

"And you reported the body at two forty-seven."

"I guess so. I wasn't looking at my watch."

"But The El Rancho is ten minutes away from here," Barwell said. "What took you so long?"

I blushed. Bad habit.

"We stopped for a while," Jeff said.

"I wanted to rest," I added, quickly.

Barwell looked from me to Jeff and back again.

"Had you been drinking?" he asked.

"You could say that," I agreed.

"So there were times on the beach when you might not have been aware of everything going on around you," he said. "Would that be fair to say?"

"Maybe," Jeff said.

"We would have noticed if a man with a gun walked by," I said. "And we didn't."

Barwell glared at me. He didn't like my attitude. That made us even.

"Let's get this straight," he said. "You left The El Rancho at around two or shortly after. You walked to, and then along, the beach, and arrived at the Gulf Vistas Hotel approximately forty-five minutes later. Right?"

I nodded.

"Why did you go on the beach? The road is more direct."

"Neither one of us was driving because we knew we were going to be drinking," Jeff explained.

"But why the beach?" Barwell persisted.

"Because it was pretty," I said. "The moon is full."

Barwell looked disgusted. Obviously not a romantic.

"Pretty," he repeated. "Also pretty cold. Not a great night for walking."

"If you're Canadian, this isn't cold," I said. "So we're just doing the tourist thing. That isn't a crime, is it?"

He glared again.

"While you were on the beach, you stopped, to rest," he said, emphasizing the word, "but you heard nothing. How long were you *resting*?"

"I don't know," I said. "A few minutes, I guess. I didn't have a stopwatch on me."

"And you are sure you heard or saw nothing."

"Yes," Jeff said.

"Wait, Jeff," I said. "I just remembered. I did hear something. I thought it was a car backfiring."

Barwell looked at me like I was a specimen in a jar.

"You thought it was a car backfiring," he said.

"I guess maybe it was a gunshot," I said, resisting an impulse to titter.

"And what about you, Mr. Glebe? Did you hear the same sound? And conveniently forget about it?"

"I guess so," Jeff said.

"You guess so. And do either of you guess you might be able to tell me when you heard this sound?"

"I don't know," I said.

"Neither do I," said Jeff.

"It wasn't too long after we began walking," I said. "Maybe ten minutes. So it would be ten past two, depending on exactly what time they kicked us out of the bar."

Barwell flipped through his notebook for a moment, then sighed.

"You two are going to be useless witnesses in court," he said.

"Well, I've never heard a gunshot before," I said. "I thought it was a car."

Barwell closed his book and got up.

"I may have more questions for you. You'll be hearing from me. And you should come in tomorrow, or later today, to give a formal statement. Ask for me."

He went out the back door.

I looked at Jeff. He looked at me. I shrugged.

"I guess we are dismissed," he said.

"He could have offered us a ride home," I said.

"I don't think generosity is his style."

CHAPTER

10

It was past 5:00 when we got back to our hotel. I was both exhausted and jangling from the coffee we'd been drinking. I also felt numb. Jeff paused for a moment outside the entrance.

"About earlier," he began.

"Let's just forget about it," I said. "It wasn't the world's best idea."

"It seemed like one at the time," he said.

"So it did," I said, putting my arm around his waist. "But I think we're lucky it didn't go any further."

"Yeah." He kissed me in a brotherly fashion, somewhere between my right eyebrow and my cheek.

We were crossing the lobby when Julie, the night clerk, called to us.

"Where have you guys been?" she asked. "Some man has been looking for you all night. I put him in your suite, Jeff."

"What?"

"Some guy from Toronto," Julie said. "He said he

was a friend of yours, Kate. He waited in the bar for you until it closed. Then he asked me to let him in your suite, but I wouldn't. When he said he knew you, too, Jeff, I figured it would be safer to put him there."

"Does this guy have a name?" Jeff asked.

Julie looked through some papers on the desk.

"Yeah, wait," she said, "I've got it here somewhere."

"It wouldn't be Andy Munro, would it?" I asked.

"Yeah, that's it," she said, surprised.

Jeff and I looked at each other and began to laugh, a tad hysterically.

"Surprise!" I said.

"Let's go wake him up," said Jeff.

"No, give me your key. I'll handle this one alone."

"You sure?"

"No, of course not," I said. "But there's only one way to find out, isn't there?"

"I'll wait down here, then," he said.

"I won't be long."

Jeff's place was exactly the same as mine, if messier, on the floor above. I let myself into the room and turned on the entrance-hall light. Andy was on the bed, fully clothed, snoring. He looked so sweet that tears came to my eyes.

I tip-toed across the room, sat on the edge of the bed, and kissed his cheek. He opened his eyes immediately, looking confused, and made "where am I?" kinds of noises until his eyes focused. Then he smiled.

"This is a nice surprise," I whispered into his neck.

He sat up and hugged me. He smelled stale,

slightly sweaty, with an overlay of scotch. But mainly he smelled like Andy, a welcome and arousing scent.

"Happy birthday," he said.

"Thank you."

"I think it's a bit late for that, isn't it?" he asked. Letting go of me, he turned on the bedside lamp, and squinted at his watch. "Where the hell have you been?"

"It's a long story," I said. "Let's go to my room."

I held off explanations until we were there, and I'd called down to the front desk to let Jeff know he could have his room back.

"I've got to get some sleep," I said, stripping off my clothes.

"What about my explanation?" Andy asked, helping me.

"I don't know where to begin," I said. "Let me tell you about it in the morning."

"Considering the circumstances," he said, climbing into bed, "I guess I can wait."

"I can't," I said, putting my arms around him.

I closed my eyes and felt the familiar textures of his body, the silk of his belly, the sandpaper of his beard, so well-known to me, and so exciting after being apart. But it wasn't quite right. We were just out of synch, and I couldn't erase the residue of horror and guilt from the night's various events. Afterwards, Andy began to apologize. I stopped him.

"Tomorrow," I whispered. A moment later, I was dead asleep.

I woke up at around noon, with a jolt. I had been dreaming about blood. Andy was sitting at the kitchen table, drinking coffee and reading the paper.

I opened the curtains on a miserable day, stumbled to the stove, and poured myself a cup. Normally I drink tea to start the day, but this morning I needed the caffeine blast.

"About time," Andy grumbled, but his eyes were smiling. "I've read everything in all three papers, including the Sun Coast Deaths. Average age, eighty-seven."

"With the weather today, probably a few will drown," I said, crossing to the table for a hug.

The rain streamed down the window panes, and the wind whipped palm branches against the glass.

"Some Florida vacation," Andy said.

"How long have you got?"

"Just the long weekend. I'm going back Monday afternoon."

"That only gives us three days," I said.

"And you've already wasted half of one," Andy replied.

"I'll call the office. Maybe they'll give me some time off. No, I'll call Jeff first, see if he'll cover for me. No, maybe I should let him sleep a little more."

"Stop dithering, Kate. Call. Invite him up for a coffee. Then you two can explain exactly what you were doing all night long together."

"Hanging out with cops, what else?"

Andy looked mildly astonished.

"Hey, I haven't seen you for ten days. I have to get my fix somehow," I said, picking up the phone.

"If I woke you up, I'm sorry," I said, when Jeff answered. "You are ordered to present yourself at suite 413 for a cross-examination about our whereabouts last night. Staff Sergeant Munro presiding. Coffee's on."

I hung up and went back to the table.

"Here's the sports section," Andy said. He never reads it unless I point out a story I'm particularly proud of. It's another reason we get along.

"Actually, I want the front," I said. "Crime news."

I went through the news sections quickly. There was nothing about Lucy's murder, which didn't surprise me once I thought about it. It happened too late for the morning deadlines. I was picking up the sports section when there was a knock on the door.

"I'll get it," Andy said.

"What's the matter, are you afraid we'll whisper in the hall to get our stories straight?"

"Something like that," he smiled.

Jeff looked a little bleary and awkward, with his long pale legs hanging out of a tattered pair of navy blue jogging shorts. His tee-shirt was faded and frayed. He did look cute.

"Morning," he said.

"Good morning, Jeff," I said. "I trust you slept well."

"As well as could be expected," he said.

"Me, too," I said.

Andy handed Jeff a cup of coffee and motioned towards the sugar bowl and milk carton on the table.

"This court is called to order," I said, in a deep voice. "His Honour Judge Andy presiding."

"All I want to know is where you were last night, while I was enjoying the pink and grey hospitality of the Flamingo's Nest Lounge," Andy said.

"I'll confess," I said. "The evidence is all over the place. It's a fair cop."

I got up and went to the wastebasket.

"Exhibit A," I said, holding up the empty half-bottle. "Champagne. Bought in honour of my birthday, and consumed on these premises.

"Exhibit B," I said, holding up the other empty champagne bottle. "More champagne. Bought in honour of my birthday by my co-accused, Jeff Glebe. Consumed on these premises by my co-accused and myself, while I opened my birthday presents."

"Exhibit C," I said, crossing the room and posing with the leopard-skin nightie. "Birthday present, sent from Toronto by one Sally Parkes. I forgot to wear it last night."

"It's an improvement over that flannelette job with the pink flowers," Andy said, approvingly. Jeff laughed.

"I only wear that when I have a cold," I said, indignantly.

"Or when you have your period, or when we've had a fight, or when you've had a bad day at the office, or. . . "

"Enough, enough," I said. "You don't have to trot out all our intimate secrets. Jeff will be embarrassed."

"Don't mind me," he said, smiling smugly. "I'm enjoying this."

"I'm not," I said. "Let's get on with our tale of last night."

I poured myself another coffee and sat down.

"After champagne and presents, Jeff was kind enough to take me out to dinner at an intimate French bistro . . . "

"Which I'll charge to the *Planet*," Jeff said. "I'll call her Stinger Swain."

"Thanks a lot," I said. "Then, after our duck *à l'orange*, we went to a not quite so elegant roadhouse, where we drank long-neck Lone Stars and tequila by the shot and danced the Texas two-step, because there are some men in this world who actually enjoy dancing," I said, getting in a small shot at Andy, who is terpsichoreally impaired.

"Finally, after they closed the bar on us, we strolled home along the moonlit beach telling each other tall tales."

"Everything she has told you is the truth," Jeff said, putting his hand on his heart.

"Wait a minute," Andy said. "You strolled on the beach for four hours?"

"Oh, yes," I said, "I forgot one thing. When we got to the hotel around the corner, we found a corpse on the beach."

Andy didn't quite spit out his coffee.

"And, of course, the cops kept us hanging around while they did all their police stuff," I continued. "So that's the story. Are you satisfied?"

I got up again and went to the phone.

"Jeff, I'm going to call Jake. Can I beg you to cover for me for the next couple of days? Andy's here until Monday night. They probably won't want that much."

"No problem," Jeff said.

"I'll owe you one."

"Don't think I won't collect."

Jake grumbled about it, but gave me the time off. The pages were full of hockey playoffs, and another columnist was in Arizona looking at the Cactus League baseball camps, so Jeff would only have to file one column a day on the Titans. He left to see what he could scare up at the training camp in the rain. I put on the leopard-skin nightie.

CHAPTER

11

It rained all day, giving us a good excuse to stay in. We called room service for club sandwiches and beer for lunch at 4:00, and played for the gin rummy championship of Western Florida. I won. Andy sulked. I made him feel better.

At 6:00, the phone rang. Detective Sergeant Barwell, sounding quite miffed, wanted to know why I hadn't been in to sign my statement. I explained about my unexpected visitor, which he didn't seem to think was much of an excuse.

"How soon can you get here?" he asked.

"Just a minute." I put my hand over the receiver and explained the situation to Andy. He grimaced.

"I'm not standing in the way of a police investigation," he said. "You'd better get it over with."

"You come with me, and we'll go out to dinner after," I said, then turned back to the phone.

"We'll be right down. Has Jeff Glebe been in yet?"

"He just left," Barwell said. "Do you know where the police station is?"

I didn't, so he gave me directions. Half an hour later we parked in front of the small stucco building, a wing of the municipal offices, modern and totally lacking in character. The door set off a beeper when we entered, which got the attention of a fat, bored-looking policeman sitting at one of half a dozen desks that crowded a room too small for the furniture.

He closed the dog-eared thriller he was reading and, marking his place with one pudgy finger, ambled over to the reception wicket. We told him our business. He glared and punched a button on the intercom.

"She's here," he said. "And she's got a guy with her."

Detective Sergeant Barwell's disembodied voice told us to hold on a minute. The fat one didn't move.

"You her lawyer?" he asked Andy.

"Do I need one?" I replied. "Is tardiness an indictable offence in Sunland?"

Andy looked pained. My inability to resist cop-baiting is not one of the things that endears me to him. I was saved from further transgression by Barwell's arrival. He was dressed a bit better than the last time I saw him, in a shiny lightweight suit. His tie, which was an ugly swirling mess of blues and green, was firmly done up. He looked very anal-retentive.

"Asked him if he was her lawyer," Fat Cop explained. "He didn't answer."

"I didn't have a chance," Andy said, smiling and putting his hand out to his counterpart. "Andy Munro. Not a lawyer."

"No," I interrupted. "He's one of you."

Barwell took his hand, warily.

"What do you mean by that?" he asked.

"I think she's trying to tell you that I'm a member of the Toronto police force," he said.

"He's a staff sergeant in the homicide squad," I said, since he wouldn't blow his own horn. "As in boss of the team. Like you."

"And what do you have to do with this investigation?" Barwell asked. Fat Cop was taking it all in, his head swivelling back and forth like someone at a tennis match.

"Nothing at all," Andy said, quickly. "I'm just visiting my friend Ms Henry."

Barwell grunted.

"I would have thought you would understand the importance of getting the statement," he said.

Even Andy bristled at that.

"We're here, now," he pointed out.

"Right," Barwell said. " You stay right there. Miss Henry's coming with me."

He took me by the arm. I pulled away from him.

"What's the matter, you think I plan to make a break for it?" I asked. "I don't need to be dragged around."

"Kate," Andy said, in a warning tone, then he turned to Barwell. "You could treat her with a little more respect."

"I don't know how you conduct your affairs up there on the big city homicide squad in Canada," Barwell said, "but down here in the sticks, we expect cooperation from our witnesses. You might even say we demand it. She treats me with respect, she gets it back. She treats me like shit . . . "

78

He let his voice trail off. Andy was getting tight in the jawline, an early warning sign I'd learned to watch for.

"Let's just cool it," I said. "I apologize for not having come in sooner, okay? I'll be pleased to cooperate, so let's just go and get it over with."

Barwell held the door for me. I thanked him and went through. He led me into a small office that was obsessive in its tidiness, and sat down behind his empty desk. There was another desk in the room, and a large cork board. Pinned to it were a series of photographs of Lucy Cartwright's body, taken from many angles. I chose the straight-backed chair that put me with my back to the view.

"What was your relationship with Lucy?" Barwell asked.

"I knew her, slightly," I said. "I've seen her around the ballpark every spring for the past few years."

"You like her?"

"Not particularly," I said. "I thought she was shallow, and she didn't exactly give women sportswriters a good name."

"Are you one of those women who goes into locker rooms with naked men?" Barwell asked.

"That's one part of my job," I said, trying to keep cool.

"You like looking at naked men?"

"Depends on the circumstances," I replied. "And what has this got to do with the investigation?"

"What kind of family do you come from, anyway?"

"My father was a minister before he retired," I said.

"And he lets you go around with naked men?"

"First of all, nobody 'lets' me do anything. I choose to do what I wish. Secondly, I don't 'go around with naked men,' as you put it. I interview athletes, some of whom are undressed. That's my job, and I do it very well. And finally, although it is none of your business, my father happens to be very proud of me."

"No better than a whore, if you ask me," Barwell said.

"Luckily, I'm not asking you," I said. "Could we please get on with this statement you are supposed to be taking."

"Lucy Cartwright was a slut," he said. "Everyone in town knew that."

"I think she was just a lonely, insecure person who didn't know any other way to feel like she was appreciated," I said, surprising myself.

"I think she got what she deserved," Barwell said.

I couldn't think of anything to say. I just stared at him, wanting to get out of the room.

"That doesn't mean I'm not going to find the guy who did this," he added.

"Why do you say guy? It could have been a woman, couldn't it?" I asked. Barwell looked at me strangely.

"Could have been you," he said. "Told me yourself you didn't like her."

"There are a lot of people I wouldn't invite over to my house for dinner," I said, "but I usually manage to stop short of blowing them away."

"Tell me what you saw last night," Barwell said, pulling his notebook out of his pocket.

"Again?"

He just stared at me. I guessed I didn't have any choice.

"We were walking down the beach and I saw what I thought was someone asleep on one of those sunbathing chairs by the bar in back of the hotel. When I went to see if the person needed any help, I realized it was Lucy and that she had been shot."

"Why did you think she had been shot?"

"There was blood all over the place," I said.

"How did you know she hadn't been stabbed?"

"I didn't know," I said. "It didn't occur to me."

"Didn't occur to you," he echoed. "But you said you didn't hear a shot when you were on the beach."

"Well, I guess maybe I did, without realizing it. Maybe that's why."

"The backfire."

"Yes."

"You didn't recognize it as a shot."

"How could I? I don't know from guns."

"And it took you forty-five minutes to get from The El Rancho Roadhouse to the Gulf Vistas Hotel."

"Yes."

"Why?"

"Because we stopped for a while."

"To rest," he said, sarcastically.

"Yes."

"Cut the crap," he said, slamming his notebook down on the desk. "Your buddy has told me all about it."

"All about what?" I bluffed.

"You tell me, and I'll see whether you tell the truth."

"I told you last night. I was feeling a bit dizzy, so I sat on the beach for a while. We talked."

"What did you talk about?"

"What has that got to do with anything?"

"I'll decide what's relevant around here," Barwell said, loudly.

"I don't really remember what we talked about," I said. "We were singing, I remember that. We talked about work stuff, maybe, and about my birthday. It was my birthday last night."

"And you look like you're a bit old to be gallivanting around drunk in the moonlight, if you ask me," Barwell muttered.

I didn't speak.

"And way too old to be screwing in the sand," he added.

"You pig," I said, and stood up. "I don't have to listen to your stupid insinuations. Just give me the damn statement to sign. This interview is over."

"Sit down," he shouted back, then spoke more quietly. "You probably don't want your boyfriend out there to hear what you do when you are on the road with your friends from work."

"I have done nothing I'm ashamed of," I said. That wasn't absolutely true. I hate ending sentences with a preposition.

"Did you notice anyone else on the beach when you were there?" Barwell asked, going back to his notes.

"Nobody."

"After you found the body, what did you do?"

"We went into the hotel and called the police."

"Have you remembered any additional information that you would like to add to your statement of last night?"

"No."

Barwell opened his top drawer and brought out a piece of paper. He got up and handed it to me.

"Read this and sign it," he said. "Then you can leave."

He walked out of the office.

CHAPTER

12

I didn't speak to Andy until we were back in the car. Then I exploded.

"How can you work with guys like that?"

"Hey, don't blame me for some cracker asshole with a badge," he said.

"He's a cop. You're a cop. What's the difference?"

"You're a baseball writer. Bill Sanderson's a baseball writer. What's the difference?"

"All right. Point taken. But I don't see how you can stand being in the same business as some of those guys."

"I can't," Andy said. "So I ignore them. I would suggest you do the same."

"That won't be hard," I said. "You're right. I'm wrong. I'm sorry."

"You want to put that in writing? I'd frame it and hang it on my wall."

"You wish," I laughed. "To commemorate the one

and only time in our entire relationship that you've been right about anything."

"Exactly," he said. "And now that you've got your sense of humour back, can we go eat dinner?"

Later, over coffee in a big, noisy, seafood restaurant with a reputation better than its food deserved, we came back, more calmly this time, to the subject of police.

"I don't like guys like Barwell any more than you do," Andy said, "but I can understand why he is the way he is. When you spend your life fighting people who don't play by the rules, you learn that trusting people can get you into trouble fast. There are a lot of cops who think that anyone who isn't another cop is potentially a crook."

"Yeah, and half of them are crooks, too. I bet Barwell's corrupt."

"Maybe. It happens," Andy said.

"And he's a power freak," I went on. "That's something else a lot of cops are."

"But not me," Andy said. "If I were, I could never be involved with you."

"And you are also smarter than other cops."

"Some," he admitted.

"And better looking."

"Indubitably."

"And sexier."

"Probably."

"So what are you doing being a cop?"

We were heading into territory we had ploughed often before.

"I like to catch the bad guys," he said. "I love my work. I'm good at it. And I won't stop doing it."

I took his hand.

"And one of these days one of the bad guys is going to win," I said. "I don't want to lose you."

"And I could teach school and get hit by a bus, Kate. I could be a gardener and get struck by lightning, too. My job isn't that dangerous. And I'm smarter than the bad guys, remember?"

"I know, but you'd be just as dead killed by someone stupid."

"Enough," he said, kissing my cheek. "We will grow old together, I promise. As long as you don't get hit in the head by a foul ball or something."

Tears came to my eyes. Embarrassed, I looked down at my plate.

"You're such a wimp," Andy said, smiling. "I don't know why I hang around you."

I laughed and wiped away the tears.

"Let's get out of here," I said.

On the way to pay our bill we passed through the bar, where we were hailed by a table full of drunken sportswriters, Jeff among them. I went over to them, and crouched down by Jeff's chair.

"What the hell did you tell Barwell we were doing on the beach?" I whispered.

"Nothing," he said. "Talking."

"That bastard," I said, then told him what I had gone through.

"It was pretty much the same with me," Jeff said. "He's not a very nice man."

"I think that would be your basic understatement," I said, getting up. Andy came to the table and joined me.

"Sit down, sit down, have a drink," said Bill Sanderson. "You can tell us all the gory details."

"I think I'd rather forget about it," I said. "But what were the ballplayers saying?"

"They were pretty freaked out," Jeff said. "The cops were over at the park talking to them."

"That's right, she was at their party," I said.

"Did you tell Barwell about that?" Andy asked.

"No, he didn't ask about it, and I forgot. Oh great. He probably thinks I was hiding it from him."

"They found her car parked over by their condos," Jeff said. "That's how he found out."

"Maybe that's one reason he was so hostile tonight," I said, to Andy.

"Probably," he agreed. "That wasn't very smart of you."

"How did I know? I saw her there in the afternoon."

"It seems that nobody admits to seeing her after about midnight," Jeff said. "She might have been with one of the players, or maybe she just wandered off. Anyway, no one's saying."

I glanced at Andy. He looked bored.

"We've got to go," I said. "I'll see you Tuesday."

Andy and I drove home in silence. The restaurant was several towns up the coast from Sunland, and I was tired. I had dozed off by the time Andy parked in front of the hotel, right next to the Sunland police cruiser. The dreaded Barwell was sitting in the driver's seat, drinking coffee from a cardboard cup.

"Oh, no," I said. "Not again."

"Maybe he's not here for you," Andy said.

"Maybe if we ignore him he'll go away."

"Fat chance of that," Andy said, opening the door.

Barwell looked at us and rolled down his window. "You lied to me," he said.

"And good evening to you, too, Detective Sergeant," I replied.

"Why didn't you tell me about the Cartwright girl being at the ballplayers' condo?"

"Because you didn't ask," I said. "I'd forgotten about seeing her there, as a matter of fact. It was in the afternoon. I didn't know there was any connection between that and her death. Do you think there is?"

"Seeing as how that was the last place she was seen alive, it's a mighty tempting conclusion to draw," Barwell said, turning off his car and opening the door.

"And since her car was still parked there, it's a pretty good bet," he continued. "So maybe you and me should have a little talk about some of those players you're protecting."

"Right now?"

"This is a murder investigation, Miss Henry. Murder investigations aren't a nine-to-five job."

"All right, you might as well come inside, then," I said.

When we got to the lobby, I glanced into the bar. It was nearly empty.

"Let's talk in here," I said. I wanted to avoid having Barwell contaminate my suite with his foul presence.

"Fine with me," he said.

"I think I'll come along," Andy said. "If I won't be in your way."

"Suit yourself," Barwell said, and walked into the bar. I shrugged at Andy and followed him.

"Bring me a beer, Marge," he called to the bartender, and led us to a corner table.

"You want anything?" he asked as we sat down. I declined. Andy went for a beer.

"Let's name names here," he said. "Which players was Lucy going around with?"

"I don't know," I said. "I'm the baseball writer, not the gossip columnist. I don't concern myself with their private lives. But from what I've heard, she's been involved with a lot of them. And not just the Titans, either."

"She was a slut, like I said before," Barwell grunted. "Everybody in town knew that. But only you know which players are the real bad ones. Plus I hear you helped catch the guy who killed a couple of players up there in Toronto a while back."

"That was Andy's case," I said. "I just got caught in the middle. I don't think I can help you. I can't imagine that one of the players could be involved."

"What have you got?" Andy asked.

"Fuck all," Barwell said. "No weapon, no motive. She was shot at close range, twice, with a .38 revolver. No signs of struggle. Miss Henry and her friend are the closest witnesses we've got and they say they didn't hear or see anything. We figure she was killed at about one-thirty in the morning."

"And no one saw her after midnight," I said.

"Where did you hear that?"

"I was talking to some of the sportswriters," I said.

"What about Ms Cartwright herself?" Andy asked. "Is there any drug involvement, or any old grudges around?"

"She smoked grass is all," Barwell said, "There

are a lot of old lovers, but none of them stand out as a suspect. People didn't necessarily approve of Lucy, but they mostly liked her."

"So you've got a lot of hard slogging ahead of you," Andy said. "I don't envy you. It's the worst kind of case. I had one like it a few years ago. Turned out to be some kind of religious nut, one of those anti-abortion demonstrators. He said that God had told him to destroy the harlot."

"We've got plenty of those around here," Barwell said.

I had to put up with an hour of shop talk before we finally left. Cops have bonds that go deeper than personalities, and the two of them had a good old time sucking back the beers and reminiscing about all the criminals they had outsmarted.

Later, when we were going to sleep, I questioned Andy about his ability to cosy up to such a creep.

"He's not so bad," he said. "Besides, look on the bright side. I don't think he's going to give you a hard time anymore, now that he realizes what a fine fellow I am."

CHAPTER

13

Andy was right. Barwell apparently forgot about me, and we were able to enjoy the last two days of the long weekend without any interruptions. We drove down the coast to a bird sanctuary on Sunday, which was a page out of the tourism brochures, so warm and sunny that just breathing in the soft air can make you giddy. The whole body opens up and relaxes, as if a winter's worth of chill has finally been driven from the marrow of your bones.

Andy got all thrilled about some sandpipers he'd never seen before. They all look alike to me, beige and boring. I like the birds that sing in the trees and have pretty colours, not the ones that skitter around the sand looking silly. Andy's been a birder for years, though, and I'm just an apprentice weirdo. Still, it was nice to be away from chain restaurants and highways, in a place of quiet and peace and pleasures that weren't manufactured. It must have been very beautiful in this state before the people got here.

Monday afternoon, which came awfully quickly, I drove him to the airport in St. Petersburg and waved him on his way, wishing I was going with him. I don't like spring training. Florida is too bland for me, and the baseball that's played here is meaningless. And Andy's leaving just reminded me how often we would be apart during the long season ahead.

So I was feeling pretty sorry for myself again when I got back to the hotel and found the message light in my room blinking imperiously. Jake Watson was loooking for me, and Gloves Gardiner had called. Strange. Players seldom call reporters. I answered Jake's call first. He wasn't at his desk, but the switchboard tracked him down for me in The Final Edition, the bar on the first floor of the *Planet* building.

"Holiday's over," he said. "I need something for tomorrow on the arrest."

"What arrest?"

"Domingo Avila's."

"What for?"

"For murdering that girl."

"Lucy? You're kidding."

"It happened at three this afternoon."

"I was at the airport."

"Well, find out what you can and file as soon as possible," Jake said.

"What's Jeff doing on it?"

"I can't find him either. If you see him, tell him to call. Figure out between you who's going to write what."

I hung up, then dialled Gloves's number. He answered on the first ring. There were other voices in the background.

"Can you come over?" he asked. "We've got to get Dommy out of jail, and we need your help."

"Give me a few minutes," I said. "I've got to file a story first. Tell me what you know. Like, when and where was he arrested?"

"At the ballpark. We were playing an intersquad game. They came and got him. Took him away in handcuffs."

"Like, right off the field?" I asked. "Sorry if I sound ghoulish, but I need to know for my story."

"They didn't even wait until the inning was over. The cops told me to call time out, and went into left field and got him."

"What inning?"

"Jesus, Kate. The fourth. Top of the fourth."

"Did they take him in his uniform?"

"No, they let him change into street clothes."

"Do you know who made the arrest?" I asked.

"Big, cold-looking guy. In good shape."

"Troy Barwell? Detective Sergeant Barwell?"

"Could be."

"I'd better call him."

"Are you going to be able to get over here tonight? A bunch of the guys are here, and we want to do something about it."

"An hour, maybe two, depending on whom I can get to fast."

"Okay."

"Just one more question."

"Yeah?"

"Did you keep on playing?"

Gloves laughed.

"What do you think? Olliphant had us back out

there in fifteen minutes. One of the other kids played left."

"I'll see you later, if I can."

"We'll be up. Call when you are done."

I got off the phone and called the police station. I got right through to Barwell.

"I don't have to say anything to you," he said.

"Just give me a quote I can use in my story."

"We are satisfied on the evidence that we have the right man," he said. "The apparent murder weapon was found in Mr. Avila's possession, for one thing."

"He had it on him?"

"We found the weapon in the accused's apartment. It was an illegally obtained firearm. We have charged him with illegal possession as well as murder in the first degree."

"Has he got a lawyer yet?"

"The team has contacted an attorney, yes," Barwell said. "He is meeting with the accused at the moment."

"Could I have his name?"

"Buford Whitehead."

"Buford? It sounds like something out of a Tennessee Williams play."

"Mr. Whitehead is a very well-known attorney in this area," Barwell said. "The Titans are sparing no expense."

"That's something," I said.

"I beg your pardon?"

"Nothing," I said quickly. "Will there be a bail hearing? What is the next step?"

"He will appear before the judge at the Pinellas County courthouse in St. Petersburg for an advisory hearing tomorrow morning at ten," Barwell said.

"I'll be there," I answered. "I assume that the press is allowed."

"Welcomed, Miss Henry. A free press is a cornerstone of our democracy."

"Thanks," I said. "I'll see you there."

Next, I called the office of the Sunland weekly newspaper, the *Sentinel*, and found the editor, Cal Jagger, at his phone. I had met him a couple of times at the ballpark, and he seemed to be a guy who would know what was going on. He remembered me and told me what he knew. For one thing, that Whitehead was the most high-profile criminal lawyer on this side of the state, working out of Tampa, the nearest big city. He specialized in murder and other big lost-cause cases.

"I tell you, Kate, when Buford Whitehead defends someone, they get the best defence there is," Jagger said. "There are some that call him the criminal's best friend. Cops and state attorneys don't think much of him, but I'll tell you one thing, he sure keeps them on their toes."

"I guess," I said. "Do you have a morgue down there, by the way? Any back issues?"

"Sure, what do you want?"

"Some background on Lucy Cartwright. I knew her from around the ballpark, but I don't really know much about her past. I thought I'd come by and take a look."

"As a matter of fact, I've just pulled the file for a story I'm doing for this week."

"Is there much?"

"Not really. Some pictures – you know those in happier times' shots papers run when someone has died."

"Yeah, like the wedding picture of the couple in the murder-suicide pact."

"You got it," he chuckled. "Anyway, there's one of the high-school cheerleading squad about five years ago, a graduation picture, and another one when she won a prize at the tri-county science fair."

"When was that?"

"Let's see. When she was in junior high. She won second prize for a genetics project, breeding gerbils."

"She was a good student, then?"

"You sound surprised," he said.

"Well, I guess she didn't strike me as a very serious person," I admitted.

"She was top of her class all the way."

"How come she didn't go to college?"

"Money. Her mother works as a bartender in one of those raw bars on the beach. Her stepfather wouldn't give her the money to go to college, so she got a scholarship at the junior college in St. Pete's, and worked for the magazine to make money for books."

"You seem to know her pretty well," I said.

"I know most people in this town," he said. "That's my job, isn't it?"

"Can I come and talk to you tomorrow about this?"

"Sure," Jagger said. "It's press day, but we'll have put the paper to bed by around seven. I've got beer in the fridge, and I'll be able to give you my full attention. If that's not too late for you. We can probably help each other out."

"I'll see you then," I said.

CHAPTER

14

It took longer than the hour I had promised Gloves, but I got a pretty good story written and filed and was at the condo by 10:00. The group gathered included most of the players I would expect to be concerned about a team-mate in trouble: Joe Kelsey; second baseman Alejandro (Americanized to Alex) Jones; Atsuo Watanabe, the Japanese shortstop; right-fielder Eddie Carter; and Tiny Washington, first baseman turned broadcaster. Eddie's wife, Clarice, was there, too.

"Thanks for coming, Kate," Karin Gardiner said, after she let me in. She is a small, natural-looking woman, a little chunky, with short, curly dark hair, a wide, imperfect smile, and fewer diamonds than most player wives.

"They're framing the kid," Gloves said. He looked like Howdy Doody without his moustache. I tried not to laugh.

"Maybe so," I said. "But I don't know what we can do about it."

"Someone has got to stop them," Gloves said. "And we're all he's got."

"What makes you so sure he didn't do it?" I asked.

"I know Domingo since he was little boy," Alex Jones said, in his heavily-accented English. "His mother is my mother's cousin. They lived with my family, lived in my house, the house I built for my mother, when Domingo was only small. It is like he is my baby brother. I know he would not do such a thing."

"No violence in his past? No trouble in the Dominican? Drugs? Anything like that?"

"This boy is just interest in one thing, baseball,"

"Not quite, Alex," I said. "With respect. He is also interested in women."

"He is a man," Alex shrugged.

"But he was involved with Lucy last season," I said, "when he was playing here."

"Who said that?" Joe Kelsey asked. "The police?"

"No, she told me that, come to think of it. The day before she died."

"If everyone who slept with Lucy was a suspect, the jail would be full," Eddie said.

"I'd be the only one outside," said Joe, to some laughter.

"Plus, the police told me it was his gun that did it," I said, trying to keep them to the point.

"His gun, maybe, but who knows who fired it," Tiny said.

"True enough," I said, "but who else could have? Who knew about his gun?"

"All of the people living at the condo, for one thing," said Clarice. "Dommy showed it off."

"How did he get it into the country?" I asked.

"He got it here," Eddie said. "He just got it last week."

"Why would he get a gun, if he wasn't planning to use it?" I asked.

"Domingo always had a gun at home," Alex said. "Everyone does. For the banditos. He felt safer with a gun."

"How did he get it? Aren't there laws against just going and buying a gun?"

"In Florida? Don't be ridiculous," Joe said. "This state has got the loosest gun laws around."

"Actually," Gloves said, "he couldn't get it legally here. Because he's a foreigner. He had to get the gun privately."

"And you know who get it for him?" Alex asked, then answered. "Lucy, she's the one."

They let that one sink in for a while.

"So, someone else who knew Lucy would have known about the gun, too," Tiny said.

"How could Lucy get a gun?" I asked.

"Who knows," Gloves said. "She might even have bought one at one of the gun shops. Anyway, she knows a lot of people in this town. She would know where to get a gun."

"What can we do to help Dommy?" I asked. "He's got a lawyer already."

"We can find the real killer," Gloves said. "Or, rather, you can find the real killer."

"Me? What are you talking about?" I laughed and looked around the room. Everyone else was serious.

"You're the only one with any experience," Joe

explained. "You found out who killed Sultan Sanchez and Steve Thorson. You found the guy who was killing those kids in Toronto last year."

He spread his hands in a gesture that seemed to signify that there was no argument to be had.

"Come on, get serious," I said. "I didn't find those guys, they found me. I'm not a detective. I just bumbled around after the story and tripped over the killers."

"That's all we want you to do this time," Gloves said.

"Kate, he's such a nice kid," Karin Gardiner said. "I know he couldn't have done this. But everything is against him. If we don't help him, nobody will."

"We'll pay you," Eddie said, insulting me. I dismissed that idea with a flap of my hand.

"It's not the money. It's just that I don't know where to begin. I'm not a private eye."

"No, you're not a private investigator," Gloves said. "But you are an investigative reporter, right? It's just like any other story, except you'll do more investigating than reporting this time."

"We'll all do anything we can to help you," Joe said. "But we can't go to all the places you can. We have to practise, for one thing. You can imagine how Olliphant reacted."

I could.

"I don't know how I can help," I said.

"If you interviewed her family and friends you might find something out," Tiny said. "God knows you found out all sorts of stuff about me when you wrote that article a few years ago. Some things I didn't even remember myself."

"You're good at that, Kate," Joe said. "You have an excuse for prying."

"I could do that, I guess. I don't know if it would do any good, though."

"It's better than doing nothing," Gloves said.

"I don't even know if I could get the paper to let me off the regular stuff," I said.

"Just say you'll try," Karin said. "Please."

"I can do that," I agreed.

I wrestled with it all the way home. I would be lying if I said the idea didn't attract me. I like playing detective, no matter how much I deny it. On the other hand, I know that any success I have had in the past has had more to do with luck than talent.

The decision was taken out of my hands the next morning at 8:00, when Jake Watson called.

"You've been seconded," he said. "Orders from the managing editor. He wants you to go on the murder story so he doesn't have to send down one of the police boys."

"What about the Titans?"

"I've put Jeff on them for now."

"He doesn't mind?"

"He's grumbling a bit, but he hasn't got much choice," Jake said. "He was going to go over and cover the teams on the other side of the state for a week, but I think our readers can do without another series of features on how unhappy they are at the Yankee camp, don't you?"

"They'll manage."

"Okay. So I can tell them you'll be filing something for the front section later today?"

"What do they want?"

"Just follow the story. I think they want a piece on the dead girl for the Saturday paper. You'll be dealing with Shelley Mitchell on the city desk. Call her."

"Okay," I said.

"Do good, kid," he said. "Make us proud. The honour of the sports department is at stake."

"Thanks for the added pressure, Jake."

"Don't mention it."

CHAPTER

15

The Garden of Memories Funeral Home, from which Lucy would be making her final journey, was a low-slung, modern, beige stucco building, with Moorish arches and stained-glass windows of an objectionable abstract design. Jeff and I parked my car in the shade of a large palm and crossed the closely cropped lawn to the front path. We checked the notice board for directions to the Serenity Chapel, where Lucy's family was receiving friends.

Walking down the thickly carpeted corridor past other reception rooms, I tried to avoid staring at the corpses propped up in their satin-lined coffins while, all around them, the living sipped cups of coffee and chatted. Most of them – the quick and the dead – were elderly, although in one particularly sad room, a couple who looked to be still in their teens sat on either side of a tiny coffin, with a baby displayed on pink velvet.

We signed the guest book outside the Serenity

Chapel, took a deep breath, and entered. It was a large room, decorated in reassuring, muted tones, with paintings of classical northern gardens on the walls. There were perhaps a dozen people standing around in in three or four groups. What conversation there had been stopped, and every head turned our way. I put on my most polite and respectful smile and waited for one of them to speak.

A tall young man approached us, looking uncomfortable in a tie and suit that was too small for his muscular bulk. He was slightly menacing, with long hair tied back in a pony tail and a fu manchu moustache.

"Are you looking for someone?"

I introduced myself and Jeff.

"We worked with Lucy," I explained.

"I'm Ringo, her brother," he said.

Ringo?

"I recognize your names," he added, after we shook hands.

"Did she mention us?" Jeff asked.

"You're the ones who found her."

"As a matter of fact, we did," I said. "We're very sorry for your loss."

The words came out easily enough. I was, after all, a minister's daughter, and used to this kind of event.

"The bastard who did it," her brother said. "I'd like to get my hands on him."

He clenched his fists, as if to demonstrate the degree of his ferocity.

"I wonder if you would introduce us to your mother," I said. "We would like to express our condolences."

Ringo shrugged, then led us to a pale, drawn woman sitting on a couch by the (mercifully) closed coffin, nervously smoking a cigarette.

"These here are the folks who found Lucy, Mom."

I ignored his tactlessness and conveyed our sympathies.

"I'm June Hoving," she said, then indicated a wiry older man with thinning hair and glasses, who stood beside and slightly behind her, one hand resting on the back of the couch.

"This is my husband, Dirk. He was Lucy's stepfather."

We shook hands, then June invited me to sit next to her. She was big-boned and strong-looking for all her grief, but had a tense and distracted air. Her hair was pulled back into a severe chignon, with a few wisps escaping around her forehead. She wore a plain navy-blue dress belted at her slender waist.

"Lucy talked about you," she said. "She told me that you were her role model."

Oh lord, I thought.

"I'm honoured," I said.

"She always wanted to be a reporter," she continued. "Her father was a writer, too. I guess that's where she got it. I was glad she had ambitions."

She stopped, then stared bleakly ahead. Her eyes were red. She lit another cigarette.

"I understand that you two were very close," I said.

"Like sisters," she said. "Everyone said we were like sisters. We were friends, best friends."

"I know this isn't a good time," I said, "but I would like to write a story about Lucy for my paper in Toronto. Would you be willing to do an interview with me?"

She glanced at her husband, who was talking to Jeff.

"I guess that would be all right," she said. "When do you want to do it?"

"Whenever is convenient for you."

"The funeral is tomorrow," she said. "I could do it the next day."

"That would be Thursday," I said.

"If you say so," she said. "I don't know one day from another anymore. They're all the same. Rotten."

"I'll call you Thursday morning," I said.

She gave me her address and phone number, which I wrote on the flap of my cigarette pack.

"Is there anyone else you think I should talk to?" I asked. "Perhaps one of her friends?"

"She didn't really have many close girlfriends," her mother said. "I think maybe they were jealous of her."

"Was she seeing any man regularly?"

"Not lately. She didn't want to get too serious about anyone. She saw what happened to me. I got married when I was eighteen, and I haven't had much of a life. I always told her there was plenty of time for getting married and having a family."

She got that haunted, bleak, look again.

"Oh, shit, here I go again," she said, and started to cry. Her husband bent down to pat her shoulder, and glared at me. I got up.

"We'd better go," I said to Jeff.

Before we had a chance, there was a small commotion at the door. Lucy's brother was scuffling with a large, shambling man, who was as intent on coming in as Ringo was on keeping him out.

"She was my damn daughter," the man shouted, shaking off Ringo's hands. He stood, a bit unsteadily, and glared around him. The room fell silent, tense.

Lucy's father, if that's who it was, was a mess. Clearly, he was drunk. His face was blotchy, his grey hair, thin on the top, hung in greasy tendrils to his shoulders. He was dressed in faded jeans and a work shirt, embroidered long ago with flowers and a peace symbol.

"My own damn daughter," he repeated, more quietly.

Hoving began to move towards him, but June stopped him with a hand on his arm.

"I'll handle this," she said, then crossed the room.

When the old hippie saw her coming, he began to cry.

"It's okay, Ringo," she said to her son, coming between him and the other man.

"What are you doing here, Hank?" she asked. "You shouldn't have come."

"My baby," he sobbed, and threw his arms around June. She winced, then embraced him and patted him on the back like a child who needed soothing.

Dirk, the second husband, started towards them, but a shake of her head over Hank's shoulder stopped him.

"Get your father a cup of coffee, Ringo," she said, then led the man to a pair of armchairs in the corner of the large room farthest from the coffin. They sat down, and conversation, which had stopped again, picked up, loud and embarrassed. Jeff and I left, unnoticed.

It was pouring rain. We ran to my rental car, splashing through puddles. Jeff slammed the door and slumped in the passenger seat.

"I hate that stuff," he said.

"Which particular stuff do you mean?"

"Coffins. Strangers. People crying."

"Oh, that stuff," I said. "Not my favourite, either, but it's not too bad. You get used to it."

"What do you make of the father?"

"The hippie? He looks pretty screwed up. I bet there's an interesting story there, though."

"The stepfather is a different kind of dude altogether," Jeff said. "He's so straight."

"I guess June didn't want to make the same mistake again. Only a fool marries a poet twice."

"What makes you think he's a poet?"

"June said Lucy's father was a writer. Assuming that's the guy, he doesn't look like he writes copy for the Chamber of Commerce. Maybe he's a songwriter, but I put my money on poet."

"Or the Great American Novel," Jeff said.

"The first chapter, max. He's probably blown his attention span away with drugs and booze. I doubt that discipline is one of his virtues. I'll have to check him out."

"Where are we going?"

I looked at my watch.

"I'll drop you off. I've got a meeting in half an hour with a guy from the *Sentinel*."

"The local rag?"

"He knows where all the bodies are buried."

"In a manner of speaking," Jeff said.

CHAPTER

16

A small elderly woman wearing a flowered dress and a pale blue sweater was looking at the sky and fussing with an accordion-pleated plastic rainhat, just inside the door of the storefront *Sentinel* office. She was talking away as I approached, perhaps to me.

"Will you look at that? This is the worst spring I can remember."

"I'm looking for Cal Jagger," I said.

"It's good for the gardens," she said, still peering at the rain, tying on her hat with a bow under her chin. "But not for my rheumatism."

"Cal Jagger?" I asked.

"He's inside, dear," she said, then turned and called gaily back into the room. "Company, Mr. Jagger! And I'll be on my way, now."

A man of about my age came out from behind the counter. He was tall and slightly stooped, with a strangely old-fashioned haircut, parted almost in the middle. It looked good with his rimless glasses, striped shirt, and bow tie. It was as if he had watched Gregory Peck playing the part of a small-town news-paper editor one too many times.

"Thank you, Estelle," he said, patting her shoulder. "I don't know what I would do without you."

The tiny lady beamed, and bustled out the door into the parking lot, pausing for a moment to tap on the glass in front of the gerbils in the pet shop next door. She caught me watching.

"They get lonely at night," she said. The editor and I shared a smile.

"Kate Henry, I think," he said.

"Guilty."

"Come on in. We're wrapped up for the week."

He held up the counter-top for me to pass into the main office area, where a couple of men and one woman were covering their computer terminals or cleaning off their desks. It was a cheerful, friendly place, with tourism posters and community notices tacked to the walls. We went through it into a small, messy office in the corner. Jagger cleared some papers off the second chair.

"How would a beer go about now?" he asked.

"It would go grand, thank you. I've just come from the funeral parlour."

"That'll give you a thirst every time. Just let me let the rest of the staff out, and then we can talk."

I looked around the room while I waited. It was messy enough to be a journalist's. There was an old upright typewriter on the desk, as well as a computer. A tall bookcase held reference books, style guides, and some of the better books about the craft. There were various plaques on the walls, and framed photographs which told me something of the man: Cal Jagger with chubby wife and red-haired children, one of each, in a studio portrait; Cal Jagger with large fish; Cal Jagger with Gloves Gardiner, on the golf course; autographed photo of Jimmy Carter; autographed photo of Jimmy Buffett. There was a faded snapshot stuck into the frame of one of the Chamber of Commerce certificates of commendation.

I got up and looked at it. It was a piece of ancient history, a faded candid shot of a group of laughing young people in tie-dyed gear, sprawled under a palm tree on the beach. I tried to recognize a younger version of Jagger beyond the hair and love-beads.

"Beach Blanket Blowout, 1970," a voice behind me said. I jumped. Jagger was grinning and holding out a cold can.

"Sorry, I didn't mean to be nosy," I said, taking the beer. "Is one of these wild and crazy young guys you?"

"Third from the left," he said, laughing. "The one making the peace sign."

"Amazing."

"You're wondering how that disreputable kid turned into this straight and respectable good burgher of Sunland, right?"

"Something like that," I confessed. "It's none of my business, of course. Besides, I've got some pretty embarrassing photographs of myself in that same era."

"It was the standard story. I wanted to defy my conservative parents with their small-town attitudes. I ran all the way to Chicago to write the Great

American Novel. Got a job on the *Tribune* to pay the rent. Settled down a bit. Discovered I liked a few middle-class comforts. Reconciled with my parents just before my dad died, and came home to run his newspaper. Met my high-school sweetheart on the street one day, married her six months later, and we have lived happily ever after."

"And the Great American Novel?"

"Right up there," he said, pointing to a cardboard box tied with string on the top shelf of the bookcase. "I take it down and look at it from time to time. The world may have to be denied the pleasure."

"No regrets?"

"No. Not for any part of it."

"What about the other people in the picture? Ever see any of them anymore?"

He came and stood beside me, gulped some beer, and pointed at the kid with his fingers making horns over his neighbour's head.

"This one was killed in Vietnam," he said. "The day before his tour was up. This one died of a drug overdose over in Miami. This one runs a liquor store in Saint Pete's. Bobby is a real estate broker now, almost as respectable as I am. I've lost touch with Dwayne completely. Last I heard he was out in California, working in a bar band. And this one is still the same."

He looked at me.

"Except for the fact that his daughter just got murdered. This is Hank Cartwright, Lucy's father. She was born about when this was taken."

"He was at the funeral parlour."

"Sober?"

"I doubt it," I said, then told him the story. He shook his head.

"Poor Hank. He's a sad case. I hardly ever see him anymore, but I think about him sometimes. Do you ever wonder why it is that some of us came through the drugs and craziness and out the other side and others didn't?"

"Yeah, I do sometimes. I've got friends like that in my past, too."

"It haunts me. Take Hank. He was bright and talented, probably the most talented of the whole bunch of us. But he just pissed it all away. He crossed the line and never came back. It was a real waste."

"What does he do now?"

"He gets by," Jagger shrugged. "He still deals drugs on a minor level, I think. Grass. There's a blues band he sings with sometimes. He drives cab when he can keep himself straight for long enough. He lives in a trailer in a friend's backyard. His friends look out for him."

"He was a writer once?"

"Still is, for all I know. He was a poet; a good one. A bit self-indulgent, now that I look back, but he was young. He was a wizard with words, though. Better than me, that's for sure. He just never took it to another level."

"So you were a friend of June's too?"

"Yeah, we were like a family, about a dozen of us, before I left," Jagger said, then went behind his desk and sat down, gesturing towards the other chair for me. "I still see her from time to time, at the restaurant. She was doing okay, too. Until this. I'd better go and see her later."

"She looked like she could use some old friends," I said.

"Yeah, I'll go see her. Garden of Memories, right?"

I nodded.

"Well, enough about my misspent youth," Jagger said. "How can I help you?"

"Just some background. I'm doing a weekend feature on Lucy. I guess you know that one of the Titans has been arrested."

"Yes. Pretty convenient for Troy Barwell."

"What do you mean?"

"It's handy having a stranger to charge. A foreign stranger, particularly. A *black* foreign stranger's even better."

"Barwell's a racist?"

"You've met him. What do you think?"

"I'm from Canada. I thought he was pretty unpleasant, but I try to avoid stereotyping all Southerners as ignorant bigots."

"Don't bother. He's a racist and a bully. I've known Troy Barwell for twenty years. He used to go out with my youngest sister when they were kids. Even then, he was a brute. We were all glad when she came to her senses and dumped him."

"I can't imagine anyone wanting to go out with him."

"He was a big wheel in high school. He was the star of the baseball team, he was good-looking, his daddy was rich. Quite a combination. He still has no trouble attracting women."

I shrugged.

"The charm escaped me. Is he married?"

"Divorced. Twice. Rumour is he beat both of them up a bit."

"Somehow, I'm not surprised."

"But you're not here to listen to gossip about our police force, right?"

"Right. I want to talk about Lucy. I don't know how well you knew her."

"Pretty well. She used to work for me, part time."

"When was that?"

"A few years ago, when she was still in high school," Jagger said. "She was a bit scattered, but not a bad worker."

"Tell me about her. You're the first person I've talked to who had anything nice to say about her, outside of her family."

"Well, she was bright, as I told you, despite that airhead act. She was starved for approval, for affection."

"I could see that."

"There was no such thing as too much praise for Lucy Cartwright. I always had to be really careful. At that point in her life she would burst into tears if she thought she had done something wrong."

"She always seemed pretty thick-skinned to me."

"That came later. I'm no psychiatrist, but I think that her father leaving had a lot to do with it."

"When did her parents split up?"

"I guess she was about four when he went to jail the first time. That pretty much ended the marriage."

"What did he go to jail for?"

"Drugs. He was dealing pretty heavily."

"You said that was the first time. How many times have there been?"

"Hank's always getting in trouble. A couple of

short stretches for theft, the drugs that one time, and a bunch of petty stuff. Drunk driving, drunk and disorderly, busting up a bar when they wouldn't serve him. Things like that."

"Did they have any kind of continuing relationship?"

"I don't think so," Cal said. "June once told me he always broke promises to the kids. Missing birthdays and things like that. Lucy had given up on him by the time she was seven."

"So your theory is that her promiscuity was based on losing her father's love?"

"Yeah, I guess that's too pat," he admitted.

"No, there might be something in it. How promiscuous was she? I've just heard all the rumours about her with the ballplayers. Are they true?"

"Probably. She didn't go around with any of the local boys in recent years. A lot of them tried. Her last local boyfriend was the kid she went steady with in high school. He was pretty cut up when she began to date the ballplayers. He tried to commit suicide when they broke up."

"That's terrible."

"He was a bit unhinged to begin with. He's been in and out of the state hospital ever since. Arnie was his name. Arnie Bonder."

"What about her mother? How did she get by?"

"June? She's done the best she could. I don't think Hank ever gave her a penny of support, but she's raised those two kids pretty well."

"And the brother? Is Ringo his real name?"

"June was pretty nuts about the Beatles," Cal laughed. "She originally wanted to call him Sergeant

Pepper. Lucy was named after Lucy in the Sky with Diamonds."

"Acid has a lot to answer for in this world. What does Ringo do?"

"He's a mechanic. He works at the company where his stepfather works, Trucking for Jesus."

"Trucking what?"

"Haven't you seen their trucks around? They're born-again truck drivers. That's what Dirk does. He brought Ringo into the fold a few years ago. I'm not sure he's completely settled down yet, if you want to know the truth. I think he accepted the Lord to get a job. But Dirk's happy."

"Trucking for Jesus?"

Cal laughed.

"They've got murals painted on the sides of their eighteen-wheelers. Jesus in the passenger seat, the co-pilot."

"When did she remarry?"

"Five or six years ago, I guess."

"Is she born-again, too?"

"I guess so, but she's not obnoxious about it."

"And she works in a bar?"

"Like I said, she's not obnoxious about it. I think she went through it just to please Dirk, but she lives her life pretty much the way she wants to. He's on the road a lot."

"She fools around?"

"No. But she doesn't sit at home praying, either."

"I'm seeing her day after tomorrow. It's interesting to know all this."

"I think you'll like her. She's a smart, strong woman."

"She seemed a bit deluded about her daughter, though."

"I doubt if she really is. She's not naïve. But she always supported her, no matter what. She paid Lucy's rent when Dirk kicked her out of the house."

"Why did he do that?"

"He's not a big one for racial mixing," he said. "When Lucy started dating blacks, they got into a pretty big row about it. I thought June was going to move out, too, for a while, but she stayed."

"I thought you said she was smart."

"Dirk is basically a good man. He's solid. And around here, his attitudes aren't that unusual."

"I'm beginning to figure that out," I said. "Listen, I might as well be straight with you. I'm working on the assumption that Avila didn't do it. How does that strike you?"

"Not too far-fetched," he said.

"Did Lucy have any enemies that you know of? Anyone who could be capable of shooting her?"

He thought for a moment.

"Only about half a dozen," he said.

CHAPTER

17

I guess I showed how startled I was. Jagger laughed.

"I'm exaggerating a bit," he said. "But there is a dark side that lurks behind Sunland's tidy middle-class stucco façade. There is an under-class, even in paradise, and there are some pretty tough characters around."

"How would Lucy be involved with them?"

"She grew up with them. She went to school with the kids who went on to become thugs and drug dealers and petty criminals. And that's not all. There are some among the proper folk who are capable of being judge, jury, and executioner when it comes to someone who behaves the way Lucy did."

"They'd shoot her for sleeping around?"

"Especially with blacks," he said. "The father of that boy I told you about, who tried to commit suicide, is widely rumoured to be active in the Ku Klux Klan. Axel Bonder would like nothing better than to get rid of Lucy and frame Avila."

"Wait a minute. How could he get hold of the gun? It was in Avila's condo."

"Last I heard, he manages the property."

"Oh. That's convenient. And what about his son?"

"I think he's safely in the bin these days, but I'm not sure. There's another suspect for you. Then we have the other ballplayers. One of them might have had a grudge. You'd know about that better than I would."

"I don't know anything about their private lives."

"You could find out. Maybe one of them found her presence embarrassing."

"You don't murder because you're embarrassed."

"It's a possibility. So's Barwell, by the way. He took a run at Lucy this spring. She humiliated him pretty badly."

"How so?"

"She got a bit drunked up at The El Rancho one night and told the wrong people that Barwell is rather spectacularly under-endowed."

"Uh-oh."

"Gave him a brand-new nickname, too. Dick Teensy."

"This did not go over well, I assume," I said.

"First person who called him it to his face got punched out. Now they just call him that when he's not around."

"I didn't realize that Lucy had a cruel streak."

"Not really," Cal said. "It wasn't exactly the kind of information that's easy to keep quiet."

"Hey, I can't wait to pass it on myself," I admitted.

"It is pretty funny," Jagger said. We both laughed.

"This isn't really getting us anywhere, though," I said. "I wish I knew what my next step should be."

"What do you mean?"

I decided to trust Jagger. I explained something of my history in matters of murder and what the players expected of me.

"I can't convince them that I'm not some sort of super private eye."

"But you are good at digging out stories," Jagger said. "That's the first step."

"I know. But I'm just worried I'll let them down."

"Could you use some help? I have got a few skills of my own going rusty on this little rag."

"Are you sure you can spare the time?"

"I haven't got much on for the next few days, anyway. Let's see how it goes."

"Do you know this lawyer, Whitehead, who's representing Dommy?"

"Better, still. I know the woman who works with him. She'll be doing most of the preliminary work, anyway. We'll get her on the team, too."

"I think I saw her at the arraignment this morning," I said. "A dark, kind of homely woman?"

"That's Esther," Cal said, picking up the phone. "I'll call her right now."

Half an hour later we were sitting in a back booth in a crowded, comfortable, beachfront bar with a cold pitcher of beer on the table between us.

"This is the place where June works," Cal said. "I thought you'd like to see it. Before Esther gets here, let me tell you a bit about her."

"Okay."

"She's about thirty. Grew up here, then went away to college, and graduated from Harvard law school. She is very, very bright and more than a little bitter. Growing up in Sunland Jewish and, as you said, homely, wasn't the greatest for her. She never really fit in. I was surprised that she came back here to practise law. I always figured that she would end up in the north somewhere. But I think she wants to be near her parents. There also might be a bit of 'in your face' in her attitude. Success isn't bad revenge, you know."

"She works with Whitehead in Tampa?"

"Yes, that's the other reason she came back. He's the best there is around here. And God knows, there's lots of work for a criminal attorney in these parts."

"How do you know her?"

"She's a friend of my wife, Beth. They were both on the board of a women's shelter a few years back, and became very close. She's like part of the family now. The kids love her."

Before we had a chance to get any further, Esther Hirsch arrived. She was short and over-weight, with dark curly hair slightly flecked with grey. She carried an oversized, bulging purse, and wore jeans and an old sweatshirt. Imprinted on the front was a comic-strip frame of a woman with one hand held to her brow, and a word bubble reading "Oh, my God! I forgot to have children!" She obviously had a sense of humour.

She also had a firm handshake and a warm smile. She greeted me, then gave Jagger a big smacking kiss.

122

"Ve haff to stop meeting zis way, my dahlink," she said, in a deep, comic slavic accent. "Your vife vill be getting suspicious."

"Like I was telling you, Kate, Esther is an extremely formal and serious person."

"I can tell," I said.

"All right, what's this all about?" she asked. "Do I get to order some food first?"

We called over the waitress, who wore hot pink lycra knee-length pants and a cut-off purple tank-top which proclaimed that she had "eaten it raw at Molly O'Toole's." We ordered a couple of dozen oysters, a giant order of peel-'n'-eat shrimp, and another pitcher of beer.

"How well do you know Avila?" Esther asked.

"A bit. He's just a rookie. How's he doing?"

"Not too great. He's pretty scared. He seems like a nice kid, though."

"I think he is. And I think he's been framed. Are you going to be able to get bail?"

"Not a chance. A foreigner charged with first-degreee murder isn't considered a terrific risk to stick around."

"It's going to destroy him, being in jail," I said. "Especially after the season starts and he's completely alone."

"We'll have the crime solved by then," Cal said. "No problem."

"Which we did you have in mind?" Esther asked.

"That's why we called you here," Jagger said. "This is the founding meeting of the Jagger, Henry, and Hirsch Private Investigation Agency. Murders R Us. We're going to find the real killer and clear Avila's name."

"Forgive your friend's melodramatic exuberance," I said. "Let me explain."

I went over the whole story again.

"It occurred to Cal, and I agree, that you are well-placed to be of some assistance, if you are willing," I finished.

She thought for a second.

"Why not?" she said.

CHAPTER

18

Before the night was over, we had divided up the areas where suspects might lurk. Esther was keen to look at Troy Barwell's life. She had a criminal lawyer's traditional distrust of cops, and she thought Barwell was even worse than most. She was our contact with Domingo and also agreed to do the slogging through old court documents we might need to investigate, since, as she pointed out, she speaks and reads lawshit fluently.

Jagger was going to use his connections with Lucy's family and friends. I was going to look at the possibilities on the team. We agreed to meet in a couple of days, and exchanged phone numbers in case anything dramatic came up.

I saw Jagger the next morning, at Lucy's funeral. He was sitting towards the front of the characterless modern church, fairly close to the family, with a red-haired woman I recognized from the picture in his office as his wife. They were just across the aisle from Hank Cartwright, who appeared to be sober, but suffering. He was wearing a suit that looked borrowed, and his hair was in one braid down his back. Willie Nelson on a bad day.

Jeff and I sat at the back with a group from the ball club. Gloves and Karin Gardiner sat with Tracy Swain. The David Sloanes also attended, which surprised me. I didn't expect those two pillars of the Mormon church to have much sympathy for a woman as scarlet as Lucy.

Eddie Carter, Joe Kelsey, and Tiny Washington were in the row behind us, conspicuous in the otherwise white crowd. Hugh Marsh came with his assistant, Millie, from the dining room, and her big, red-faced husband. None of the other Toronto reporters showed up.

I did a quick count of the house, while an elderly organist slogged her way through a lugubrious rendition of "Lucy in the Sky," etc., peering through bifocals at the sheet music propped up on the little electric organ. There were about seventy-five people there, many of them young. Barwell was there, and thinking of Lucy's nickname for him took some of the threat out of his glowering. I also recognized the first cop on the scene the night we found her, the one who had looked so upset when he heard who it was. I made a note to ask Cal or Esther to check if there was some history there that we should know about. I looked in vain for any obvious murderers in the crowd.

June, dressed in black, sat stiffly between her second husband and her son in the first pew. On Ringo's left was an older couple, probably Lucy's grandparents.

The service was brief and too pat for my taste.

The minister, a stern man in his fifties, was apparently Dirk's pastor, and seemed to have had little acquaintance with Lucy. He talked about God calling her home as if he believed it. My father used to be a minister, so I went to more than my share of funerals growing up, and I've never heard a eulogy so lacking in comfort.

I was glad to get out of the stuffy church and into the glorious spring sunshine that seemed to mock the mourners as they came out the doors. I paused just outside, when I saw a police car pull up to the curb in front of the church.

I thought at first that it was there to escort the hearse, until I saw Detective Sargent, Barwell's partner, get out and scan the crowd. When he spotted his boss, he walked quickly to him and grabbed his arm. They moved off to one side, Barwell glaring as he listened. He looked both surprised and angry as he moved away from Sargent and cut through the group surrounding June Hoving. He shook her hand and spoke to her for a moment, while Sargent moved back to the car, started it up, and idled at the curb. When Barwell had finished paying his respects, he got into the car and the pair drove off with a squeal of the tires.

"What's up?" I asked.

"Huh?" Jeff said. He hadn't been watching.

"Wait here a second."

Cal Jagger and I had agreed to pretend that we didn't know each other, but when I spotted him, it was obvious he was looking for me, too. He hadn't missed the scene with the police. He made a discreet motion with his head and strolled away from the rest of the congregation, towards the parking lot and around the corner of the church. I went the other way round and met him behind an oak tree. Very cloak and dagger.

"What do you think that was about?" he asked.

"I was hoping you could find out," I said. "There's something going on. We should check it out."

"It's probably easiest for me. I'll go back to my office and make some calls."

"No. Stay here and do what you're doing with the family. Just call me as soon as you find out anything. If it's another body, at least Dommy is in the clear."

Jagger looked at me oddly. I guess it was a rather strange remark, but I've only been involved in two murder cases, and each of them had more than one victim. Why should this one be any different? It would make my life a lot easier.

"It might not even be connected," he cautioned.

"I'll bet it is," I said.

"I'll call you later. Will you be at the hotel?"

"Or you can leave a message."

I waited a few minutes after he went back, then went to join the group still gathered on the lawn. The Titan contingent was just leaving. Gloves stopped when he saw me.

"I thought you'd split," he said. "How's it going? Have you found anything out yet?"

"I've barely begun," I said.

"I wonder if the murderer was here at the funeral," Karin said, with a shiver. "That's what always happens on television, isn't it? The killer shows up to gloat."

"This isn't television, Karin," Tracy said.

"Where's Stinger this morning?" I asked. She shrugged.

"He had an early tee-off time. I thought that one of us should do the right thing."

"I'm sure the family appreciate it," I said. "How did you know Lucy?"

"She used to babysit some of the kids when she was just a teenager," Tracy said. "Stinger's and mine and David and Marie's twins."

That explained the Sloanes' presence.

"Ours, too," Karin said.

"I didn't know that. I only met her later, when she started working for the magazine," I said.

"I didn't see much of her anymore," Tracy said. "But we both think it's a great tragedy. The Lord works in mysterious ways."

I agreed and moved on, stopping to speak briefly to Tiny, Joe, and Eddie, who were starting to leave. We exchanged some small talk, awkwardly. Funerals are not an easy place to talk to people with whom you normally laugh a lot.

"I'd like to get together later," I said. "After practice, I guess."

"He'll probably keep us late because we took time off to come here," Eddie said.

"I can talk to you any time," Tiny said. "I don't have to listen to Massah no more."

"Aren't you filing a report today?" I asked.

"I'll be done that by lunchtime," he said.

"Well, well, aren't you sounding like the old pro now," I said. "I'll catch up with you at the media room, then. I want to talk to a few more people here."

"You just keep on with your investigating," he said, with a smile. "Maybe you should get yourself one of them trench coats."

"Yeah, but my magnifying glass is in for repairs."

"Catch you later, then."

I nodded and touched his arm. I had just spotted Hank Cartwright, by himself, heading slowly across the lawn to the parking lot.

I caught up with him as he was getting into his car, a broken-down Ford with a decided tilt to one side, and introduced myself.

"I'm doing a story for the Toronto *Planet* on Lucy, and I'd like to talk to you about her, if you have a few minutes."

He turned and looked at me, then smiled. Or leered, perhaps.

"Far out," he said. "The *Planet*. And you're Lois Lane."

"The newspaper was named before Superman was invented. As far as I know, none of our reporters does anything peculiar in phone booths."

"Too bad," he said, flirting grotesquely.

"Maybe this isn't a good time," I said.

"I have an important appointment."

"What time would be good?"

"The appointment is with an old friend," he continued. "I don't think he'd mind if you came along."

"If you're sure," I said, dubious.

He held the door and gestured me into the car.

"The passenger door is stuck."

"It's all right. I have a car. Maybe it would be better if I followed you."

"To the ends of the earth and back again?"

"To your appointment," I said, firmly. "My car's just over there."

"I await your return with wildly beating heart," he said, bowing.

CHAPTER

19

I hurried back to Jeff, who was talking with Hugh Marsh, and told him to make his own way to the ballpark. As I went back towards the parking lot, awkward on the grass in my high heels, I saw June Hoving pause beside the funeral car to look at me. I hoped I wasn't going to queer the interview I had set up with her by going off with her former husband.

As soon as I pulled my car up behind his, Hank Cartwright took off, in the opposite direction from the one the cortège was pointed. We went a few blocks, then pulled into the parking lot of a grungy bar called the Starlite. The placement of the building in the corner lot suggested a former life as a filling station. There were a couple of pickup trucks and a big motorcycle clustered around the door of the dirty grey cinderblock building. The small windows were high up and covered by semi-functioning neon beer signs. Put it this way. It wasn't a bar I would normally rush to frequent. I checked my watch. It was 10:30 in the morning. Not my idea of happy hour.

Cartwright got out of his car and went in without waiting for me. I followed a moment later. After my eyes had adjusted to the gloom, I saw him at the bar, a shot glass already to his mouth, supported by both hands. He downed it in one gulp. When he noticed me, he raised the empty glass.

"Meet Jack Daniels," he said, smiling crookedly. "My oldest and dearest friend."

He turned to the bartender, a hulking guy who looked about sixty. He was balding and grey-haired, with deformed ears and a nose that had been broken more than once. An old photograph of a handsome young boxer with his gloves up, hanging over the bar mirror, showed him in better days. He looked at us with a steady, distrustful gaze, his huge, rough hands resting flat on the bar.

"Another, please, Cecil," Hank said. "And whatever the lady wants. She's buying."

Luckily, I had plenty of cash, because Cecil didn't look like he would take Visa. I'd be lucky if he gave receipts. What would I call this on my expense account?

"Beer for me," I said. "Light beer, if you have it."

"No light," Cecil said. "Bud or Coors."

"Bud's fine,"I said, then turned to Hank. "Maybe we should sit at a table."

"Don't worry about old Cecil," he said. "He minds his own business."

"As long as you have the money to pay for his drinks," the bartender said, sliding my beer over and pouring Hank another shot. I put a twenty on the bar. He nodded, moved down the bar, and turned his attention to the television set, feigning fascination with Oprah Winfrey and her guests, who were discussing lesbian parenthood. He was still within earshot.

"Did you ever see your daughter?" I began.

"Every week," Cartwright said, picking up his glass with a newly steady hand. He sipped carefully, then smiled. "Every single week. June didn't know. Lucy never told her. But she came by, or found me somewhere, and she never missed a week. She gave me some money, sometimes. I didn't feel too good about that."

He raised the shot glass again, and took another careful little sip, delicately almost, savouring the fire. He closed his eyes and sighed. I waited for him to continue.

"She said it made her happy to help me out. It made me happy to see her, that's for sure."

He raised bloodshot eyes to mine.

"I wasn't much of a father when she was little. I know that. I was too fucked up. Hell, I'm still fucked up. But she forgave me for that. She forgave me for everything. She just wanted to know me, she said."

He fell silent, staring into the middle distance.

"When did you begin to get close?" I asked. He looked startled, as if he had forgotten I was there.

"About four years ago. Four years ago November, my birthday. My fortieth. She came to my trailer with a present."

He quickly drained what was left in his glass and wiped his eyes. Cecil looked a question at me. I nodded, and he brought the bottle. I offered Hank a cigarette, which he took. I lit it for him, then took one myself.

"She was scared," Cartwright said. "Real shy. Like a little animal. She gave me a book she'd made of some of my old poems she had found in the house somewhere, and some poems she had written. God, it was moving. She stayed for five or six hours. I was pretty wasted that day. It was like she was glowing, an apparition, a visitation, an angel who cupped my heart gently in her hands. She's been my special girl ever since."

"How long had it been?"

He sighed.

"If I'm honest, I'll tell you I never knew her before. At first, she was just a baby. I don't dig babies. Then me and June split up, and I couldn't get it together to see her for a while. Then June turned her against me.

"Not that I blame her," he said, and stopped, lost in his memories. After a few moments, he straightened and smiled at me.

"You know what I used to do? I used to go by her school during recess and just watch her from where she couldn't see me, my pretty little girl. I wondered how my daughter could be so pretty and nice. I told her that once. She cried. Like I told her, I never stopped loving her. I just didn't know how to do it without screwing her up. I guess I probably did anyway, deserting her, but it would have been worse if I'd been around. I really believe that. Or I used to. Now I don't know, and I never will."

More bourbon, more tears blotted on his sleeve. He took a cocktail napkin and blew his nose, then loosened his tie.

"She had talent," he said, calm again. "Damn, but she had talent. Did you know that?"

"I never really read her stuff. Sorry."

"Too bad. She could write. She had the magic inside her, and I did everything I could to bring it out. I lent her books, turned her on to writers she had never heard of. I opened up her mind. I gave her the wings to fly with. I just wanted to make sure she didn't piss it all away the way I did. I did something right for a change. Man, it felt good, too."

He looked at me.

"Don't get me wrong," he said. "She wasn't the only one who got something out of it. She straightened me out pretty good. To tell the truth, I was pretty close to losing it when she came into my life. 'Half in love with easeful death' when she came, like a nightingale, to bring me back."

I rummaged through the cobwebs in my memory of English 101.

" 'To cease upon the midnight with no pain,' " I said.

He raised his glass.

"Here's to Johnny Keats," he said. "He could fly, too."

I let another silence slide by before changing the subject.

"Did Lucy confide in you about many things?" I asked.

He looked at me slyly.

"Like what? What are you getting at?"

"Nothing. I just wondered what you talked about."

"You want to know if I knew about her sex life? Sure I did. She told me everything. She believed in an active, healthy sex life. Took after her father in that, too."

I let it lie between us on the bar. He took another cigarette from my pack, tore the filter off, and lit it.

"These Canadian cigarettes are crap," he said.

"The price is right," I said. He ignored me.

"Lucy approached sex like a man," he said, approvingly. "When she saw what she wanted, she took it. No guilt. No remorse. No questions asked. I admired that."

He laughed.

"So, she played with guys, used them. She had a great body and she knew how to get her way. So what? Haven't men been doing that with women since the beginning of time? A woman like you, you must be a feminist, you should approve of Lucy. Except you're probably uptight about sex."

I let that one lie right next to his previous remark. The bar was littered with innuendo.

"Lucy was free in her mind and her body. The Bible-thumpers and scum-suckers in this fucking town just kept trying to drag her back to their level. But she was too strong for them."

He smiled, then anger clouded his eyes.

"And then some jumped-up Brillo-head from the Islands, who wasn't worthy of her attention, did her. Shit, isn't that ironic? She was just trying to be nice to the poor lost little fucker."

He slammed his shot glass down on the bar, got off the stool, took his head in his hands, and let out a grating, wounded howl. Then he shook his head and walked purposefully past the pool table to the men's room. No one in the bar even looked up.

"Everything all right, Miss?" asked Cecil.

"He's had a tough day," I said. "His daughter's funeral."

"Yeah," he said. "I heard about it. But, a word to the wise. Most days are tough days for Hank. Don't let him fool you. And that twenty is just about used up."

I opened my wallet and pulled out a matching bill.

"Thanks for the advice," I said.

"I don't want to see any trouble."

"Neither do I."

"Good."

"Right."

He went back to Oprah. I went back to my confusion.

CHAPTER

20

I took out my notebook and made a few notes. Hank was back in five minutes. He seemed to have pulled himself together. His gait was steady, his eyes bright. I suspected he had used a little artificial assistance in the washroom.

"Gimme a beer, Cec," he said.

"Name's not Cec," the bartender said, not turning his head.

"Excuse me, *Cecil*, would you be so kind as to pour me a beer," Hank said. When it came, he picked it up, grabbed the bourbon bottle and his shot glass, and walked away.

"Come over here," he said. I got up and pointed to the money on the bar.

"I'm good for it," I told the bartender.

"It's your money," he shrugged.

I followed Hank to a corner table, away from the other pitiful customers. We sat down on mismatched chairs with rusting metal legs and torn vinyl seat covers that had pieces of foam sticking through. Mine had a distinct lean to the left.

"I want to tell you something in confidence," Hank said.

"Fine," I said.

"Off the record," he said, self-importantly.

"Off the record," I agreed. It was easier that way. If it was something I really needed to use, I could go back to him later to get it.

"I think they busted the wrong guy."

"Oh? Why do you say that?"

"It's too easy. They arrested him too fast. I can't believe the kid did it. He was too fucking grateful to her for letting him suck those tits to want to kill her. But that's not the main thing. The main thing is, it makes that cocksucker Troy Barwell look too good."

"You don't like Detective Sergeant Barwell?"

He looked at me with cold hatred in his eyes.

"I'd like to kill the son of a bitch."

"Why?"

"For what he did to Lucy."

"Are you saying you think Troy Barwell killed her?"

"I'm not saying anything about him killing her. I'm saying the motherfucker raped her. That's what I'm talking about here."

That got my attention.

"When?"

"Last year."

"Did she report it?"

He laughed, bitterly.

"Are you kidding? It was, what you call it, date rape. It happened at his place. It would be her word against his, and who would believe her?"

"Maybe you're right."

"You bet your ass I'm right," he said. "You know the scene. 'And why did you go there? What did you think you were going there for? How much had you had to drink?' Like that. Then they drag out all her history and make her look like a whore. There was no percentage in it. But she got back at him good her own way."

"Dick Teensy," I said.

"You heard about that? Pretty good, huh?"

"It was certainly catchy," I agreed, amused at his paternal pride.

"Humiliation is the best revenge."

"What a slimeball."

"Lady, next to Troy Barwell, a slug looks dry," he said, then got up to go back to the bar. He was beginning to stagger a bit. Little wonder. I hoped he would keep it together long enough to give me what I needed to know.

He came back with two more beers. I hadn't finished half of mine, but he put one in front of me anyway.

"Tell me more about Lucy. When did she start writing?"

"Before she even learned how to print, she was making up stories. She used to send me her little poems that June would write out for her. And Lucy would draw little pictures to go with them, too. It was pretty cute."

He paused.

"When she was four, I went to jail for a while,"

he said, quickly. "That's why June divorced me. But before that, she sent me Lucy's poems and stories in jail. Lucy kept on writing. Like I said, I didn't know it until four years ago."

"Why do you think she came to you?"

"She wasn't happy at home. June had married that holy roller, and he was putting the leash on her pretty good. Compared to him, maybe I didn't look so bad."

"Was that when she moved out?"

"No. That was later, when she figured out that step-daddy had more than Bible-reading on his mind."

"Meaning?"

"Meaning he just happened to catch her in the shower a couple of times. Meaning he liked her to stay home with him when June was working the night shift. Meaning that when he took the strap to her he'd come in his pants. And he liked to take the strap to her. Called her a harlot, read the Bible to her, then whacked her around, and came in his pants."

"Christ," I said.

"You gonna drink your beer?" he asked, his speech starting to slur. I shook my head.

"Help yourself."

"Don' wanna let it go to waste," he said, gratefully.

"I've got to be going, anyway. Just one more question, then I'll let you alone."

"Hit me," he said.

"Do you know which ballplayers she was involved with?"

"Ah, yes, my darlin's little weakness," he said. "She wasted her brains and that great body on any asshole that could swing a bat or throw a ball. She said they were the poets of sport. Shit. And she loved them. Young, old, single, married, black, white, Latin, yellow, plaid, whatever. If they wore stirrup socks with their work clothes, she had to have them."

He shook his head.

"She was hooked," he said. "She was crazy for baseball. Even when she was a kid. Lucy wanted to be a bat girl, but they only had bat boys. As soon as she got old enough she babysat the players' kids. When she got old enough to screw, she screwed them.

"That's why she wanted to be a sportswriter, so she could be part of the game. If she couldn't be an athlete, she wanted to get as close to them as she could. She wanted to screw them or she wanted to write about them."

He clenched his glass so tightly I thought it would break.

"She had real talent, God damn it. She could have been anything. Waste of time, waste of mind, being a fucking sportswriter. Fucking sportswriter. Jesus."

He wound down, and stared into his empty glass. He was done, gone. I stood up.

"Thank you, Mr. Cartwright," I said. He didn't look up. "You've been a big help. I have to be going to waste my mind now."

It didn't get through the fog. I went to the bar.

"Let him go through the rest of the money," I said to Cecil. "But hold back five for yourself. And I need a receipt."

He put down the glass he was drying with a questionable-looking rag and rummaged in a drawer under the cash register. He pulled out a receipt book with a carbon, the kind you can get at any stationery store, and concentrated on printing in it.

"Thanks," I said, when he handed it to me. I gestured towards Hank's table. "Will he be all right?"

"He won't cause any trouble. I'll just let him sleep it off in the back room. He's done it before."

He picked up his rag and smiled.

"And he'll probably do it again."

"Sorry to leave the mess for you to clean up," I said.

"No problem. You have a nice day, now," he said.

Florida. They even do the happy faces talk in the dives.

CHAPTER

21

I sat in my car for a moment to let my eyes adjust to the sunlight, and took deep breaths of air that didn't smell of stale beer, smoke, piss, and disappointment. I checked my watch. I had time to stop in at the *Sentinel* office on my way to meet Tiny.

Cal was on the phone when I got there. He waved at me, excited. The elderly woman whom I had seen on my last visit offered me a seat and a cup of coffee. I accepted both.

"I haven't seen Mr. Jagger have this much fun in years," she confided.

"Have you been with the paper for a long time?"

"Oh, my, yes," she said. "I began to work for Mr. Jagger, Senior, just after the war. World War II, that is. I've been here ever since."

"Then you knew Cal when he was little,"

"I first met him the day after he was born. Such a cute little tyke he was, too."

"Then can I ask you a personal question?"

"Of course, dear."

"Why do you call him Mr. Jagger? He calls you Estelle."

"Well, he's the boss. It wouldn't be proper to call him Cal. It might be old-fashioned, but that's the way I've always done it. That's what makes me comfortable."

"Fair enough," I said.

"His father called me Mrs. Burnett, of course. Cal doesn't, but he's from a different time. He used to call me Auntie Estelle, when he was little. I liked that. We never had children of our own, you see. My husband died in the war."

"You never remarried?"

"No, I'm afraid I was never lucky enough to meet a man who could compare with Mr. Burnett."

"I think Cal's lucky to have you," I said.

"So do I, dear," she said, then winked.

"You must have known Lucy Cartwright, too, when she worked here."

"Yes, I did. I can't say I approved of the way she went about things, but I think underneath she was a very kind girl. Even if she did use her wiles for what she wanted. Maybe that was her undoing."

"What do you mean?"

"Well, she wasn't very careful about who she became intimate with, was she?"

I got her drift. Sweet little old lady, my ass. Narrow-minded old bigot is more like it. She smiled at me, conspiratorially, then took my hand and squeezed it.

"I think Mr. Jagger is ready to see you now."

"It's amazing," he shouted from his office. "You're not going to believe this! Get in here!"

I went.

"There's a second gun," he said. "They found another .38 off the pier by the condo."

"But I thought they found the gun that did it."

"They probably did. But get this! The gun they found was identical. In other words, it could be Avila's, and if it is, the one in his apartment was a plant. It's the same model, and the serial number had been filed off both of them."

"I don't get it," I said.

"Bringing another identical gun into the picture muddies the waters. What if the first gun, Gun A, the one that they say is the murder weapon, isn't Avila's gun? Then you have to ask how it got into his apartment. There's only one way. The murderer put it there after he killed Lucy, then dumped Avila's gun, Gun B, into the ocean. Because the two guns looked the same."

"I'm not sure I get the importance of this, Cal."

"It changes everything, including the time frame."

"You mean the murderer could have made the switch any time between the murder and when the gun was found, when, Monday?"

"Right. A whole weekend during which someone could have planted the evidence that sent Avila to jail."

"The plot thickens," I said.

"And a lot of that time the place was empty, and the murderer knew it was empty because Avila was at the ballpark. So we're not just looking at the night of the party anymore."

"Which means that a lot more people had the

opportunity. Motive and opportunity. That's what it's all about, right?"

"That's what they say in the mystery novels."

"And speaking of motive, I've got some news for you, too," I said. "I've got at least one addition to our list."

I told him about my conversation with Hank, apologizing for stepping on his turf.

"That's all right," he said. "I was busy stepping on Esther's turf."

"With any luck, she has found something out on mine," I laughed.

"So, there was more behind the hostility between Barwell and Lucy than I thought," Jagger said. "There are some other things starting to make sense, too. The last time Hank got busted for drunk and disorderly, he took a run at Barwell. Unprovoked, apparently. Now I can see what was behind it."

"And Holy Dirk Hoving isn't quite as holy as he seems."

"Like I said before, the seamy side of paradise."

"Can you call Esther and fill her in?" I asked, gathering up my things. "The second gun might have some bearing on Dommy's defence. I have to get to the ballpark. You can get me there, or I'll call you later on. I'm going to look at the ballplayer angle. The second gun widens the possibilities, but we can't rule out the people who live there. After all, they were the ones who knew the gun was there."

The practice fields were empty when I parked at the training complex. The players were around the clubhouse, having lunch. They looked worn out.

I saw Tiny heading towards the media room and

honked my horn and waved at him. He stopped and waited for me to catch up.

"Lady, you sure do keep some low-life company," he said. "Who was that dude I saw you following from the funeral?"

"Lucy's father."

"That old hippie's her old man? You don't say. Looks like he's got some serious problems with the juice."

"Right the first time, Detective Washington," I said. "Now, let me tell you about what I've done so far."

"Hold on, now," Tiny said, holding up his huge hand. "There's nothing so important it can't wait until I've put something in this big belly of mine."

"Your belly doesn't need any more help, Tiny. It's taking on a life of its own. I'm surprised it hasn't rented itself a separate apartment."

"Now, Kate, don't you be mocking me."

"Maybe if you disciplined it with a bit of exercise now and then, it wouldn't boss you around so much."

"You can't begrudge a man the pleasures of retirement, now. Just because you're built like a fungo bat."

"Better a fungo bat than an equipment truck," I said.

"You're a cruel woman," he said. "Cruel."

"All right," I said. "In the spirit of compromise, I'll agree to eat if we can talk at the same time. And not in the media room."

"Hey, that's free lunch."

"I'm buying."

My expense account was going to drive the bean-counters crazy this week.

We went in Tiny's car, a big, roomy Cadillac, to a barbecue joint in the black part of town. We sat at a picnic table behind the parking lot and split an order of ribs that would feed most average families. I had about a quarter of them, Tiny the rest, along with a side order of potato salad. We drank giant colas out of plastic cups. I couldn't get much conversation going until there were nothing but sauce stains left on the paper plates. Finally, Tiny wiped his mouth and fingers daintily on a moistened paper towel from a foil packet, lit a cigarette, and smiled.

"That's better," he said. "Now you can make your report."

CHAPTER

22

Tiny listened closely to the stories I had heard from Cal and Hank Cartwright, interrupting me occasionally to ask questions, all his shuck and jive shelved.

"This looks good for Dommy," he said. "There are lots of other folks who had more reason to shoot her than he did."

"And if the gun was planted, it looks even better," I agreed. "But the fact remains that the people in that condo are the ones who knew how to frame him. That means, among others, that we have to know which of the ballplayers who stayed there were involved with Lucy."

"It's mainly just the rookies and minor leaguers she goes with. They stay at the hotel. They can't afford the condo."

"What about Dommy?"

"Alex wanted to look after the kid, so he let him move in. They stick together, you know. The team pays what Dommy's hotel room would have cost and Alex takes care of the rest."

"The players stay there year after year, don't they?"

"Sure. It's pretty handy to the ballpark. There's a pool for the kids. There's a pier out back for fishing, and it's near the mall for the wives."

"How does it work? Is it arranged through the team?"

"At first, it was, but now we rent them directly."

"It's a pretty good deal for them, then."

"Sure. They know that they've got guaranteed rentals for six weeks every spring. They just keep the booking open. And it's good for us, because we get a break on the rent, and don't have to hassle to find a place every year. It works good."

"You've forgotten again, Tiny," I teased. "What's this 'us' you're talking about?"

"Hey, give me a few weeks to get used to the idea, girl!"

"But is that why you're not staying there this year?"

"Maybe that's part of it. But I'm not here for the whole time, and my family is back home. The hotel is better for me."

"You've stayed before, though."

"For the last six years."

"How easy would it be for someone to get into the individual condos?"

"Security is pretty good," he said. "There's the guard at the gate. The apartments have good locks. But if you're asking if somebody already in the place could get into someone else's apartment, I don't think it would be too hard. People are in and out of each other's places all the time. Having a beer, borrowing stuff, like that. When there are people around, the places are open. You can see any strangers who come around."

"So if you belong there, no one is going to notice if you go into the wrong apartment."

"I didn't say that," he said, shifting on the narrow bench. "There are places some people wouldn't be expected to go."

"Stinger Swain or Goober Grabowski wanders into Joe Kelsey's place, say," I said.

"You got it. Or if anybody goes in for no reason. Someone might ask. I'm sitting by the pool and I see Flakey going into my pad. Well, Flakey's a nice guy, but he got no reason to be in my pad. So it would stand out, you know what I mean?"

"I should get a chart of who is living where."

"I don't know everybody. Some are in the same places, but other ones move when they have another kid or if their family doesn't come down. Karin could tell you."

"I'll go see her," I said. "Now, let's get back to Lucy's lovers. Did any of the guys in the condo have affairs with her in the past?"

"I wouldn't call them affairs, exactly," he said.

"Let's not quibble over semantics. Flings, one-night stands, blow jobs in the car," I said, impatiently. Tiny winced. He can't stand women talking dirty.

"Kate, please," he protested.

"Come on, Tiny."

"I never did, for one," he said. "By the time I got to the Titans, I was too old for that foolishness. Besides, I'm too scared of Darlene to be messing around with someone like Lucy. She got wind of it, my marriage would be history."

"Not to mention your manhood. But not all your team-mates have your remarkable good sense."

"You're right about that one. All right. Some guys I know about, others I've just heard about. Okay?"

"Sure," I said, taking out my notebook. Tiny looked at it and grimaced.

"All right. Eddie Carter, a long time ago, three years ago maybe. Alex Jones. Flakey Patterson. These are the guys I heard talking about her, anyway. I think maybe Atsuo, the Japanese kid, the way some guys were teasing him. I saw her coming out of Stinger's place, one time about two in the morning, last spring when Tracy was home having the baby. Like I said, you notice when something don't seem right."

"What about David Sloane?"

"Are you kidding?"

"Goober Grabowski?"

"That time I saw her last spring? I think Goober was there too, at Stinger's."

"I'd heard they like group stuff," I said. "It's good for sublimating homoerotic urges."

"Say what?"

"Never mind. Who else?"

"There are a bunch of guys from other teams who would know about the condo," Tiny said.

"Could you check and see if any of them have been hanging around this spring?"

"I'll see what I can do," he said. He looked at his watch.

"We'd better go," he said. "It's three-thirty and I'm meeting with my producer at four."

"Okay. I've got work to do, too."

We didn't talk much on the way back. I was trying to figure out what to do next. It was probably time to visit Karin.

Most of the players had left by the time we got to the park. Joe and Eddie were taking turns with the pitching machine in the batting cage; Olliphant had Watanabe and a couple of rookies out on the far practice field and was hitting them ground balls; Stinger and Goober were playing cribbage in the clubhouse. The equipment kids were sitting in the sunshine brushing dirt out of rows of cleats and polishing the shoes. Wet uniforms hung out on racks to dry. It was all very homey.

There were no other reporters in the media centre. I had some messages stuck to my phone. One from Andy, one from Shelley Mitchell, the *Planet* city editor, and one from Esther Hirsch.

I called the lawyer first.

"What's up?" I asked, when I got through.

"What's up yourself?" she said. "I'm just on my way to court. Want to get together later?"

"Maybe," I said. "Can I call you?"

"Sure, you've got my home number," she said. "Hey, it's great news about the second gun, huh?"

"I guess so," I said. "It's getting pretty complicated, though."

"Don't worry, we'll work it all out," she said. "I've got my clerk looking into Barwell's messy past. I'll talk to you later."

I called Shelley Mitchell next. She wanted to know whether I would be filing anything for the front section.

"I doubt it. There's nothing much going on. The

funeral was today, but I don't think it's worth a story."

"Probably not," she agreed. "But you will have a feature for Saturday, won't you?"

"That's what I'm working on," I said.

"Do you have any idea of length yet?"

"Not really," I said. "I won't be able to talk to her mother until tomorrow afternoon, which means I won't be writing it until Friday. Is that a problem for you? And is there a length you have in mind?"

"Depends on what it's worth," she said. "Maybe we can talk again after you've interviewed the mother. And I'd appreciate it as soon as you can manage on Friday. The earlier it's in, the more space I can get you. But aim for twenty-five inches, thirty, tops, unless you've really got a blockbuster."

"That's a fair target," I said. "I'll try to make it short and early."

"Thanks," she said, then hung up without saying goodbye. Mitchell lacks in the social niceties. Maybe she thinks she has to make up for her gender by being ruder than the boy editors.

I decided not to call Andy until I got back to the apartment. I found the Gardiners' number in my notebook and called Karin, who agreed to see me right away.

23

Karin and Gloves were both in. He was lying on the couch with a can of beer, watching a golf game on television. He got up and turned it off when I arrived.

"Would you like something?" he asked. "Karin can get you a beer or a soda or something."

"I'd love a coffee, if it wouldn't be too much trouble," I said.

"I'll put a pot on," Karin said.

"Sit down," Gloves said, "and tell me how it's going."

"Not until I get back," Karin called, from the next room.

"What did you think of the funeral this morning?" I asked.

"I hate funerals," he said.

"Who loves them? I thought this morning was particularly awful. If that sanctimonious creep of a minister could have gotten away with not mentioning Lucy's name, he would have."

"Maybe he didn't approve of her."

"Still, it's his job to find something nice to say. She must have been nice to stray dogs or something."

"She certainly took care of stray ballplayers," Karin said, coming back into the room. Gloves looked uncomfortable. She sat on the arm of his chair.

"But you're no stray, are you?" She put her hands around his neck.

"No, I have a rightful owner," he said, pulling one hand away from his throat and kissing its palm.

"But she was a good-hearted girl," Karin continued. "I liked her. She was great with kids, a terrific babysitter when she was a teenager. Our daughter adored her. I'm sure her sexual behaviour was just another expression of that generosity."

"That's a very enlightened attitude," I said. Karin shrugged.

"A man does it, we say he's a real super-stud. A woman does it, suddenly she's a slut. I don't think that's fair."

She paused.

"But if she had trashed around with my husband, I would probably have a different attitude."

"Well, maybe," I said. "But you would be assuming it wasn't Gloves's fault. Women seldom get men into bed against their will."

"True," she said.

"Can we change the subject here?" Gloves asked.

I turned on him.

"How do you handle it when you know about infidelity in one of the other players? Where does your loyalty lie?"

"It's their business," Gloves said.

"Yes, but you tell me," Karin laughed. "I know about all the bad habits on the road."

"Not quite all," Gloves said.

"And do you tell the other wives that their husbands are unfaithful?"

"No," she admitted. "I don't really know why I don't."

"I don't write about it, either," I said. "I see it, on the road. Married guys getting into the elevator with women."

"But why would you?" Gloves asked. "It has nothing to do with the game. You're not supposed to cover our personal lives."

"Yeah, but what if, say, I see a guy in the hotel bar at closing time, two in the morning. He is drunk, he leaves with a woman, and the next day he strikes out twice, grounds into a double play, and makes an error? Then it has something to do with the game."

"Maybe," he said. "But what if he hits the game-winning home run?"

"I'd vote for the woman on the player-of-the-game ballot!"

We all laughed.

"Anyway, enough about my journalistic ethics," I said. "I need some help."

I ran down the highlights of the information I had gathered so far, and asked them to help me make a map of who lived where in the complex. Gloves went to get paper while Karin poured our coffees.

"Let's go outside,"she said. "We can do the layout better if we look at it."

The Gardiners had one of the larger ground-level apartments in the two-storey complex, with a patio under the overhang of the upper floor's balcony. We sat at a round table looking out over the pool. There were half a dozen kids splashing in the shallow end, being watched by a glum-looking teenager, while the mothers tanned their oiled bodies. I guess they hadn't heard the news about skin cancer.

The condo was built around three sides of the pool, opening to the west, overlooking the gulf. There was a ten-foot-high wall between it and the beach, with a wrought-iron double gate in the middle.

The Gardiner's apartment was in the central wing, second from the end. There were five apartments up and five down. The side wings had three up and three down each, with stairs curving up each end of the units.

"The ones at the sides are the smaller apartments," Karin explained. "That's where the bachelors stay, or the ones whose families aren't coming down."

"Are all the places rented by Titans?" I asked.

"All but one in this building are," Gloves said, "same in the north wing over there, except for the super's place. The other wing is being renovated, so it's empty right now."

I got out my pen and drew three boxes to represent the buildings. I divided them lengthwise in halves, then made four vertical divisions in the main building and two in the side ones.

"All right," I said. "Looking from the pool towards this building, who is where?"

Karin leaned over my shoulder and pointed, indicating the first apartment on the left.

"Here is Eddie Carter and his family, then comes us, then the Sloanes. Goober Grabowski is in the next one. His family isn't arriving until next week. The Swains are on the far end. Upstairs is Jack

Asher, the new DH, and his family. The one next to him, right above us, is the retired couple from New York. Then comes Bobby Marchese and his family, next to the Costellos."

"We call that Little Italy," Gloves said.

"Kid Cooper is in the last one with his wife and new baby," Karin continued.

"Where was Dommy staying?" I asked.

"Okay, that's in the other building," she said, pointing to the corner unit. "He was in Alex Jones's place, on the bottom floor, nearest this building. Archie Griffin was next to him, then Joe Kelsey. On the second floor, Flakey lives on top of Alex and Dommy, next to Atsuo Watanabe, who sort of keeps to himself. The far one on that floor is Axel Bonder, the super."

"Who is one seriously weird guy," Gloves said.

"So I've heard," I said. "He also could have a connection to this case."

I told them about his mentally ill son, Lucy's former boyfriend.

"He is also rumoured to have a pointy hood and white sheet hanging in his closet, so framing Dommy would make him happy. And, he has access to the apartment. So I think we should check him out. Where was he that night?"

"Probably spying from behind the curtains," Karin said. "He's a real whatchamacallit. Voyeur. He always waits until there are a bunch of us out sunbathing before he does the pool and garden work. I can't remember if he was around that night."

"And aside from him, it's just the team staying here?"

"Right now, yes."

"And last week, when the murder happened?"

"Well, there were some outsiders at the party," Gloves said. "Most of the players were here and some brought local girls as dates."

"Including Lucy," I said.

"Yes, including Lucy," said Gloves.

"Was she here as a date?"

"I think she was doing an interview and was sort of asked to stay."

"Who by?"

"I guess Dommy and Glen Milhouse," Karin said.

"My competition," Gloves said.

"He's a cute guy," Karin teased.

"Who was she mainly with?" I asked.

"I wasn't keeping track," Gloves said.

"I was," interrupted Karin. "She was flirting with everybody, and Dommy wasn't happy about it. Although I hate to say it. But he was sulking, while she danced with other guys, especially Glen."

"Was there anything else?"

"Go ahead, sweetie, tell her," she said to her husband.

"Okay, I'd better," Gloves said. "There was kind of a scene when she was talking with a group of guys and their wives. She was asking Tracy Swain about their little girl and Stinger lost it. He was screaming at her and calling her all sorts of names."

"I thought he was going to hit her," Karin said. "All Lucy did was ask when her first birthday was."

"What happened then?"

"Goober grabbed Stinger and got him out of there. Lucy went back to dancing."

"That was pretty cool of her," I said.

"She seemed to think it was funny," Karin said. "I asked her if she needed anything, but she said she was fine."

"What time did this happen?" I asked.

"I wasn't paying attention to the time, but it was pretty late," Gloves said. "Everyone was pretty much out of it."

"Especially Stinger," Karin said.

"And Lucy," countered Gloves.

"Would it have been after midnight?"

"Maybe," Gloves said. "We went to bed not too much later."

"So you didn't see Lucy leave? Or see Stinger again?"

"No, as far as I know, Goober took him to the beach to cool off."

"But I saw Goober again, honey," Karin said, urgently. "Remember? He was throwing up in the garden when I went to the kitchen to get ice water for you."

"And Stinger wasn't with him?"

"No. I didn't see Stinger at all."

"It doesn't necessarily mean anything," I said.

"But that was around the time Lucy got shot," Karin said.

"What was?" asked a new voice. We looked up.

"You keep playing detective, one day you're going to get into trouble," said Stinger Swain, standing not two feet away in his bathing suit, with a towel around his neck.

"It's a waste of time, anyway," he continued. "The little spic did it. No question. She was showing him up. He had the gun. Maybe smoked a little too much reefer, had a few too many beers, and he snapped."

162

He sighted down the barrel of his right index finger.

"'Kapow," he said, then blew away imaginary smoke. "Goodbye Lucy."

CHAPTER

24

We all tried to ignore the remark, but Stinger kept rolling. He couldn't let it alone.

"You can't say she wasn't asking for it. And those Dominicans have got the big macho-attitude. She should have known better than to jerk his chain that way."

"Leave it alone, Stinger," Gloves said. "This is none of your business."

"It's none of her business either," Stinger said, then turned to me. "You should stick to writing your stupid articles, keeping the assholes in the stands coming back for more. But not you. You gotta go where you don't belong and get in and and stir it up. You're just all bent out of shape because one of your little bobos got in trouble."

"Well, you're right about one thing," I said. "I don't think that Dommy killed Lucy. But that's not because of any special relationship you seem to imagine I've got with him."

I have a terrible tendency to get pompous when I get mad.

"He's not one of Katie's Cuties? Don't shit me."

"What are you talking about?" I was getting mad.

"Wait a minute," Karin said. "You're way off base here. Kate's a fair reporter."

"Thanks, Karin," I said. "But don't waste your breath."

Stinger laughed – a sarcastic, incredulous sound.

"Fair to your old man, maybe," he said. "Fair to that faggot Joe Kelsey and his girlfriend Eddie Carter. And her darling Tiny Washington. She likes niggers. And all the Dominicans. They're niggers and spics, even better. She's *fair* to the pitchers because she thinks they're smarter than us. But the day she gives me any good ink, is a day I'm never going to see, because I won't kiss her ass like the rest of you do."

Gloves stood up and put his arm around the third baseman.

"Hey man, I didn't think you cared," he said, laughing. "That's what you always say. You let your numbers speak, right? Go have your swim and cool off. We got business to discuss."

"Well, excuuse me," he Steve Martined, then strolled slowly over to the beach gate and out.

"He doesn't use the pool?"

"No," Karin said. "Haven't you heard? Real men don't swim in pools. He challenges the mighty ocean every day."

"At least the not-so-mighty gulf," I said.

"Right," Karin said. "Big challenge."

"He really is a jerk," Gloves said. "It's too bad he's such a good player."

Karin glared at him, but said nothing. She began

165

to gather the coffee things from the table. I offered to help and followed her into the kitchen.

"What a pig," I said.

"You don't know the half of it," she said. "There are times I'd leave him if it wasn't for the kids."

"I meant Stinger," I said, startled.

"Oh, him," she laughed. "Him I would've left long ago."

"Why does Tracy stick around?"

"Money," she said. "Status. She grew up beautiful but poor. Being a big-league star's wife is as good as it's going to get. Wearing diamonds that spell out his name. Driving her little white Porsche with the personalized plates."

"But that can't make up for being married to someone like him," I said.

"Tracy isn't what you might call deep," Karin said. "Possessions mean a lot to her, and she doesn't want to give them up."

"Now that she has found Jesus, you'd think that she would be renouncing all those material things."

Karin laughed.

"Yeah, sure," she said, loading cups into the dishwasher. "Tracy Swain is never going to get so religious she gives away her trinkets to the poor. Last year, for example, I thought she was finally going to split. Then he bought her a bunch of jewellery and her new fur coat, and she was good wifey again. Since she's found God, though, it's worse. You never see them touch and they hardly ever speak to each other. Sometimes it looks as if she hates him, but she seems to enjoy it, too."

"Maybe he's her cross to bear."

"Yeah, the gold-plated kind," Karin said.

166

"Some kind of weird relationship," I agreed.

"Welcome to baseball."

"Come on, Karin," I said. "Gloves is a classy guy. Compared to other players, he's a prince."

"Sure, but compared to real human beings, he's still a ballplayer. The team loyalty shit really gets to me. Stinger is a good third baseman, so we have to tolerate him? That stinks."

She stopped, then laughed.

"Oh, don't listen to me," she said. "This happens every spring. We have a great winter, just the family. Then we come down here and I have to get used to the guy with the game face on. It's always hard to adjust at first."

"I'm sure."

"But you're right," she said. "And I do love and appreciate my husband. I just sometimes wish he did something different for a living."

"In not too many years, he will," I said.

"With my luck, he'll become a coach," she said.

"Right," I said. "The same schedule, with twice the responsibility, three times the stress, and about a tenth of the salary."

We both laughed and went back outside. Gloves was next door with Eddie Carter and Joe Kelsey. They called us over.

"What this? An official meeting of my bobos?" I asked. "Better not let Stinger see us."

"Clarice says the cops were here again today," Eddie said. "There was something about another gun?"

"Oh, my God," I said. "I forgot to tell you. Sorry."

I went over the story and its possible ramifications one more time.

"When did this happen?"

"I guess when we were at the funeral," Eddie said, then called his wife.

"It was just after you all left," she said. "They went to Alex's place and went through it again."

"Did they have a search warrant?" I asked.

"I think Alex told them they could. He told me about the gun after he got back from practice."

"Where did it come from?" I asked. "Do you know any details?"

"Some kid found it in the water yesterday," Clarice said. "Can you imagine such a thing? He took it home and hid it in his room. He was only ten years old. His mother found it this morning and called the police. Alex says it looks like Dommy's gun. But so did the other one."

"It was a .38, right?" Gloves asked.

"Cop gun," Eddie said. I made a note to check what the Sunland police use.

"Well, it all gets curiouser and curiouser," I said. "I've got to go, but I'll keep in touch. I'm talking to the mother tomorrow."

"Thanks for everything, Kate," Karin said.

I went past Stinger's place on my way out. Tracy was sitting at her patio table, painting her nails with purply-pink polish, while reading a matching leather-bound bible. She greeted me distantly, then went back to her project.

I walked past the steps leading up to Flakey's place to the parking lot, past the ground-floor back entrances. The guy in the coverall I'd talked to the first time I had been there was putting garbage into a large bin at one end of the building.

"Mr. Bonder?" I asked, coming up behind him. His body tensed, and he turned. His was a bitter face, lined heavily under thinning grey hair, slicked back. He wore glasses and looked to be in his late fifties. It's hard to tell with Florida faces, hides tanned in decades of sun.

"Looking for something?" he asked.

"You are Mr. Bonder?"

He grudgingly admitted his identity, and I introduced myself.

"Were you here the night the murder happened?"

"I'm always here," he said. "Except Sundays when I go see my boy."

"Yes, I heard he wasn't well," I said. "I'm sorry. He was there last week, was he?"

"Who told you?"

"I'm not sure," I said, regretting my loose tongue.

"It's none of your business, anyway, my family. What do you want? I've seen you here before."

"Last week," I agreed. "I'm a reporter for a newspaper in Toronto."

"A reporter," he said, then spat.

"I guess you see a lot of things around here," I ventured. "You know what's going on."

"I mind my own business," he said.

"What about the party last Friday?" I plowed on. "Were you there?"

"They don't give invitations to the employees," he said, dragging out the last word sarcastically.

"Did you see anything that went on?"

"I might have looked out once or twice," he said. "Couldn't sleep, with all that noise. Saw her dancing and carrying on."

"Lucy?"

"Shameless. Dancing pert' near naked, far as I could see."

"You're talking about the murdered girl."

"Some would say she got what she deserved," he said.

"Would you say that?"

He stared at a point over my right shoulder.

"None of my business."

"Did you happen to notice when Lucy left, that night?"

"Can't say I did."

"Was the gate to the beach open?"

"Not by me."

"Do you have the only key?"

"Tenants have 'em, too," he said, still looking over my shoulder.

"What about security? Who is in charge of locking it at night?"

"Last person to use it."

This line of questioning was getting me nowhere. I tried another tack.

"How long have you been the superintendent here?"

"Five years."

"So you've known some of these players for all that time?"

"Some of them."

"Do you decide who gets which apartment?"

"What if I do?"

"Nothing. I just wondered how you decide who gets what."

"Some of them have favourites. The ones here longer get their choice."

And the ones who grease the super's hand, probably.

"Which are popular ones?" I asked.

He shrugged; a small, stiff gesture.

"Ground floor for them with children and them who like a party, I guess. Upstairs for them who want some privacy."

"Are there a lot of parties?"

"Seems like a lot to me."

"With outside people or just among the players?"

"Sometimes it don't seem like they know whose apartment is whose, they're in and out so much. Not how I was brought up to be. But I wasn't a millionaire athlete, wasting my life."

This outburst of information seemed to startle Bonder. He looked around, bemused, then wiped his hands on his pants and picked up a rake that was leaning against the wall.

"I have to get back to work," he said, then put his mouth into a grotesque parody of a smile.

"It's been nice talking to you," he said.

CHAPTER

25

I stopped at the Publix on the way home and bought a frozen mini-pizza and some salad stuff for dinner. I wanted an evening alone to prepare for my interview with June Hoving, and to try to make some sense out of everything I had learned.

When I got to my room, I turned on the oven, changed into sweats, and poured myself a glass of wine before calling down for messages. I needed the fortification. There were ten of them: Jake Watson (twice), the city desk, Andy, Cal Jagger (twice), Esther Hirsch, Hugh Marsh, Gloves, and Sally Parkes.

Duty first. I called Jake, filled him in on what was going on, and told him to pass it along to the city desk. Jake said that city side was worried about photographs for the feature. I promised to get hold of Bill Spencer.

Going for pleasure next, I tried Andy, but couldn't reach him, so I called Sally and caught up with news from home. Elwy, my beloved cat, had been to the vet for an ear infection and was put on a strict diet of dry food that costs twice as much as the canned food he loves. There had been another snowstorm the day before, covering the first shoots that had come up in the garden during a three-day thaw, God's annual Toronto joke. Sally had met a promising man at a benefit for some native arts organization. It was a comforting phone call. I didn't tell her about what I was involved in. She would only worry.

When we were done, Sally passed the phone to T.C.

"Kate, why aren't you writing?" he asked. Unlike Sally, he reads the sports pages religiously.

"I'm working on a feature for the weekend," I said.

"What about Domingo Avila? Did he really do it?"

"His friends don't think so," I said.

"Why don't you catch the real killer, Kate? You can use the book I sent for your birthday!"

"Thanks, T.C.," I said. "I've got enough problems being a sportswriter."

He pumped me for ten more minutes about the fates and fortunes of the Titans under their new manager before I could get him off the phone.

"I miss you, Kate," he said. "So does Elwy."

"I miss you all, too," I said. "I'll see you in a month. Take care of Elwy, and give your mum a hug for me."

"Okay."

"Talk to you soon. I love you."

"Me too. Bye."

I put the pizza in the oven and slipped a tape into the machine. Ray Charles and Merle Haggard singing, "There's no place like home and it's lonesome in my little hotel room." Perfect.

Country music is my secret vice. I've developed the taste over years on the road with the team.

I am a radio listener, mainly. At home, it's the CBC, with its peculiar blend of information, music, and silliness, always searching for the elusive Canadian identity. American radio is another matter.

I used to go up and down the dial in each new city for a station which played tolerable music and had decent news reporting. This proved to be impossible. The music was either Top Forty rap and crap, or insipid music-of-your-life and Barry Manilow. I finally settled on country, because it's mainly melodic, tailor-made for lonely hotel rooms, and you can find a country station in every city in the American League – except New York and Boston, where I settle happily for jazz. The news reporting is pretty lousy and the announcers are right-wing, but I tell myself that I'm taking the pulse of the Real America.

I allowed myself five minutes of maudlin with Ray and his friends, then got to work.

For half an hour, I sat at my computer and made notes of all the conversations I'd had since the funeral, cross-referencing into several files: one of each of the people I'd talked with, and two general ones where I put the information that could link with Lucy's death, filed under motive and opportunity.

When the buzzer went, I checked the oven. The pizza appeared to be ready, if not particularly appetizing. I put a quick salad together and put the pizza on a plate, poured another glass of wine, and sat down. For company, I picked up T.C.'s book.

I skipped the chapters on finding missing persons and following paper trails and went to the good stuff: how to tail a suspect and how to set up a surveillance. The latter chapter advised bringing something along to pee in. That was all very well, but I wasn't sure whom to surveil. There was also a chapter on finding things out from going through suspects' garbage, which sounded intriguing, if unpleasant.

I was mercifully taken away from reading about surgical gloves, and instruments for sorting through eggshells and used tampons, by the phone. It was Esther Hirsch.

"I've just come from seeing our client," she said. "He is very grateful to you and his friends and asked me to tell you."

"Great," I said. "Meanwhile he's still sitting in jail with a bunch of real criminals, probably being raped or something."

"Calm down, Kate. First of all, I think he can take care of himself. He is a big tough boy, agreed?"

"Well, yes."

"Secondly, we have managed to get him in safe custody, away from the general population."

"That's great. Can I go see him?"

"No, it's a very restricted list. Counsel and family."

"But his family's in the Dominican Republic," I began. "No, wait a minute. Alex Jones is a second cousin or something. Does that count? Could he get in to see him?"

"Maybe it could be arranged."

"Who should he contact?"

"Just give him my number."

"Okay. What else did Dommy have to say?"

"That he is completely innocent," Esther said. "That he has no idea what happened that night. There's more. Nothing that needs following right now."

"Anything else I should know?"

"Some interesting stuff has turned up about our friend Detective Sergeant Barwell," she said. "Not to do with Lucy, but it certainly speaks to his character."

"I've got some pretty juicy stuff, too," I said. "Directly related to Lucy. But you go first."

"It's just that there have been a couple of complaints about him to the department. One was for sexual harassment of a suspect. Another for assault. He was cleared both times, but six years ago he was suspended for six months for falsifying evidence in a drug case."

"Not a good cop," I said.

"You might say so," she said. "What have you got?"

I told her about Dick Teensy and the date rape. She swore.

"Why does none of this surprise me?" she asked. "We had better get together."

"Let me get my stuff in order and do the interview with June, first," I said. "We'll do it tomorrow night."

"Why don't you come to my place for dinner?" she asked. "I'll get Cal, too. It would be a bit more private than meeting in restaurants, and I don't think you probably want us to be seen at your place."

"Good thinking," I said. "How about seven?"

"Perfect," she said.

"But don't go to any trouble," I said.

"I love cooking," she said. "It's my Jewish-mother genes. And how often do I have people to feed?"

"If you're sure," I said.

"And if you have any more stuff for me to dig out, feel free to call. I never go to bed before midnight."

"You're terrific," I said.

"Hell, no," she said. "I'm just having fun."

While I was at the phone, I called Alex and gave him Esther's number. Then I tried Andy. Still no answer. I left a pathetic message on our machine and went back to work.

CHAPTER

26

After an hour, I took a break, put on the kettle, and got into the shower, letting water as hot as I could stand it pound down over my neck and shoulders. I swear computers were designed by quack chiropractors out for business.

While the tea steeped, I did some stretches and warm-ups to work the rest of the kinks out. Then I took a mug of sweet and milky tea to the desk.

I scrolled through the information in my computer, taking notes in longhand. I don't travel with a printer, and sometimes things make more sense on paper than they do on the screen.

By 11:00, I had a bunch of paper to shuffle around, but inspiration was still refusing to strike. I was considering packing it in for the night when the phone rang. I almost ignored it. I didn't really feel like talking to Andy, because I hadn't yet decided if I was going to tell him what I was doing. I finally picked it up, trying to sound sleepy so he'd feel badly for disturbing me.

"Oh, gosh, I'm sorry," he said, but it wasn't Andy. "It sounds like I woke you up. This is Cal Jagger."

"No problem," I said. "I am just sitting and mulling."

"Mulling what?"

"Not wine. Suspects," I said.

"How many have you got?"

"At least three, so far," I said. "Troy Barwell, the rapist cop with a sexual inferiority complex; Axel Bonder, the KKK janitor with the loony son and both motive and opportunity; and Step-daddy-o just on general principles.

"Plus, I have a whole bunch of question marks about other people."

"Like?"

"Oh, Stinger Swain, Hank Cartwright, Constable Sweeney, you, an unrelated madman acting alone, none of the above, and Uncle Tom Cobbley and All."

Cal laughed.

"I think maybe you had better sleep on it," he said. "I just called to say I'll be at Esther's tomorrow. If you need me, I won't be in the office until the afternoon. I'm doing some stuff for my day job."

"Okay," I said. "I'm seeing June. I'll bring my notes to the meeting. See you at seven."

I decided to give Andy one more try. I was in luck.

"Been out carousing all night?" I asked. "Some behaviour, I say. Ignoring your hearth and home, Elwy pining for your company. But do you care? Ha!"

"Elwy's not pining," Andy laughed. "He is being

cuddled as we speak. I didn't call, because I only got in a few minutes ago, and I thought it was too late. But you're right, I was out having a good time. It's always tons o' fun at a crime scene."

"Oh. Anything interesting?"

"Not particularly. A bad one. Hooker murder in an alley behind a crack house. An empty crack house, now. Since last night, when it happened."

"How old?"

"Maybe seventeen. She was a runaway from Regina. A Native girl. Known to the guys at Vice."

"I hate that."

"They had tried to get her to go home," he said. "They got her in at Covenant House, but she didn't stick."

"So she ends up dead."

"She ends up dead. And we'll solve it the way we usually do. It's just a matter of time before one of the dealers gets picked up for something else and cuts a deal by caving in on one of his buddies."

"Her poor parents."

"Poor all of us."

"Lousy for you, too," I said.

"I'm just tired of seeing all these lives wasted."

"I wish I was there to cheer you up."

"Me, too," he said. "But hearing your voice helps. Thanks for calling."

"I wish you were here, too," I said.

We listened to the silence for a while.

"So, what are you up to?" he asked.

"Promise not to get mad?"

"You're messed up in that murder, aren't you?"

I took a deep breath.

"A bit," I said.

"Yeah, I saw in the paper that they had arrested that kid," he said. "I figured you'd get your nose in it somehow. Then T.C. asked me why you hadn't been writing, and, with the keen detective's mind for which I am so famous, I put two and two together."

"You're not mad?"

"With you, there's no use," he laughed. "If I reacted every time you did something stupid like this, I'd be in a fury half my life. Tell me what you've got."

"No, you're too tired."

"I'm wide awake. Just give me a minute to get a pen and paper. I'll take some notes."

"Thanks."

I listened to the sounds down the line; Elwy meowing indignantly at being moved, Andy answering him, then the echo of Andy crashing around in the next room.

"Be right with you," he shouted hollowly. "Don't hang up."

Then I heard the tinkle of ice cubes and he was back on the line.

"Got myself a scotch while I was at it," he said. "Now I'm all set. I'm on the couch, Elwy's back on my lap, and you have my almost undivided attention."

I fought back a wave of longing to be with him, picked up my notes, and moved the phone to the bed.

"Well, I'm swimming in motives, here," I began. "There are a whole lot of people who had a reason to hate her. Tell me something. After all the years you've investigated murders, can you get inside the heads of the suspects?"

"What do you mean?"

"Well, I can understand why some of these guys could hate Lucy, and wish she wasn't around to bug them, but I am not capable of imagining how they take the next step. Deciding to kill her, taking the gun, going out to the beach and shooting her, then calmly going on his way."

"That's because you are a basically non-violent person," Andy said. "Partly because you are a woman, partly because you are a genuinely nice human being."

"Well, thanks very much," I said.

"No, really. You don't hate. You don't bear grudges. You don't see the world as a frightening place where people are out to get you. You just sail along, bless your heart, believing that everyone is basically good and wishing that life was fairer than it is."

"You make me sound like Pollyanna," I grumbled. "Like a simp. I think there are bad people. I think some of the people I've encountered in this case are scum-sucking creeps who ought to be put away."

"Aha," he said. "There you have it. Put away, not blown away. Right? See what I mean?"

"I guess you're right."

"That's why you are having trouble."

"But you don't think that way either," I said.

"Not personally, no. But I do professionally. I have talked to enough of the other kind of people to understand how they think. To them, the world is full of scores to settle or scores to make. If someone is in their way, they simply remove them and don't think anything of it. I'm talking about the real psychopaths here. Not the domestic killings, say, where the killer calls 911 in tears or turns himself in the next day."

"So I should look at the case and imagine that I was someone who put no value on human life. Then I could take the next step."

"Something like that."

"Because if I don't, all of this stuff just seems far-fetched."

"There are lots of reasons people kill. For money and sex are two biggies. Another is in response to some sort of threat, to eliminate a perceived enemy and save one's own life."

"Self-defence, you mean."

"Not literally. I'm not talking about cases in which someone is holding a knife to another one's throat."

"You mean if I think someone is threatening my job or good name or prosperity," I said.

"Or freedom. A drug dealer suspects his buddy of being a snitch, and it's goodbye buddy. In that kind of situation, some guys run to escape the threat. Other ones stay and eliminate it."

"Gotcha. What else?"

"Revenge is another obvious one. The murderer who blows away someone who has done him wrong in some way. This ties in with the third, most psychopathic one, in which the murderer becomes the executioner. This is where we get into the real creeps. They decide that the person deserves punishment, and just do it. The guy who kills prostitutes, for example, because they are immoral. Or blacks because he doesn't like blacks."

"Well, I have to tell you, we have both types of

possibilities here," I said. "Let me call you back in five minutes."

"How come?"

"I don't want to run up long-distance charges while I pee," I said.

"I'll be here," he chuckled.

CHAPTER

27

Five minutes later, exactly, I was back on the phone, at my desk with a fresh cup of tea, a clean ashtray, and a blank page turned in my notebook. I'd turned my computer back on.

"Okay," I said, when he answered. "I'm ready to go."

"Hit me," he said. I could hear the yawn in his voice.

"Darling, you don't have to do this if you're tired," I said.

"No, no. I like hearing you play detective," he said, sounding amused. "Besides, if I have some input, you are less likely to do something really stupid and get into trouble you can't handle."

"Well, while I was in the john I thought about what you told me, and it seems that I've got some suspects here that fit into your categories, some of them into both."

"All right."

"First, and most popular in my books, is your friend Detective Sergeant Troy Barwell."

"Handy for you," Andy said.

"No, really, listen to this."

I told him about Barwell's history of violence against women, about his dishonesty as a cop, and about Lucy's rape and his subsequent humiliation.

"Dick Teensy," he said. "I like that. I may use it."

"On who? Whom?"

"You remember Bob Flanagan?"

"That jerk? You mean he's. . . ?"

"Like a thimble."

I snickered.

"Go for it," I said. "But let's get back to my problem. Did you happen to notice what kind of gun Barwell wore?"

"Sure, the same one we use."

"I thought so. And that gun is?"

"Smith and Wesson .38."

"Yes!" I said. "That's the murder weapon."

"I hate to throw a wet blanket here, but was he at this party?"

"Well, no."

"Then your theory supposes what, a chance encounter on the beach?"

"That's where it's a bit weak," I admitted.

"And how did he get the murder weapon? Do a B and E at the condo?"

"No, I've worked that out. He planted the gun during his search after the murder was reported, took Dommy's identical gun, and threw it in the ocean."

"He could have, but I think you're a bit weak on

the opportunity angle on this one. And the motive isn't so hot."

"What if she was threatening to expose the rape? It would kill any chance he had for advancement. What if he has secret ambitions to be the chief someday?"

"That wasn't Lucy's style, from what you tell me," he said. "Next."

"All right," I said. "Here's a threat motive. Dirk Hoving, Lucy's stepfather."

"How was she threatening him?"

"I'm not sure she was, but she could have. He was a prominent born-again businessman who evidently indulged in some hanky-panky with Lucy a few years ago. If it got out, it could ruin him. Maybe she was blackmailing him or something."

"Any evidence of that?"

"No. I just heard about it from her father, who isn't exactly a reliable witness."

I told him all about my conversation with Hank.

" Well, I still don't like your theory yet," he said. "It's worth following it up to see if there is any evidence of blackmail, but opportunity is weak. Have you considered the father, by the way? He sounds pretty scuzzy."

"There was something a bit unhealthy about their relationship," I admitted. "The two of them smoking dope and talking sex isn't exactly standard father-daughter stuff. But I can't see him being capable of thinking this whole thing out. His grief was real, Andy. He was suffering."

"Grief or remorse? Think about it. Anyone else?"

187

"Before I get to him, let me talk about opportunity again. You keep saying there was no opportunity with these guys, but we don't know, do we? I mean, no one admits they saw her after midnight. Anything could have happened. It could have been a chance meeting. It could have been set up. We don't know."

"No, but it's more likely that it comes back to that group at the condo," Andy said.

"All right," I said. "You're a hard sell. My next suspect has both motive and opportunity. Axel Bonder, the super at the condo. He knew about the gun, he had access to the apartments, and he had a dandy motive."

I ran down the history between Lucy and Bonder's son, as well as his racism.

"Besides, he's a really creepy guy," I said.

"Okay, but why now? This all happened, what, six or seven years ago?"

"Maybe his son has taken a turn for the worse, maybe watching her with Dommy drove him crazy. Maybe she said something to him that made him snap."

"That's all worth exploring," Andy said. "Is that all the suspects?"

"Well, no. There's Stinger Swain."

"Ah yes, your favourite ballplayer. I thought we'd be getting around to him sooner or later."

I told Andy about the scene between Stinger and Lucy, and about the rumours that he had slept with her last year.

"He had the opportunity. Maybe she was making trouble with his wife. When she mentioned the kid's birthday, he went nuts. She was giving him a little reminder that a year ago they had been to-gether. Maybe she threatened to tell Tracy?"

"Maybe. But I can't imagine that would be news to her."

"You're probably right," I said. "Karin told me they went through a bad patch last year. Maybe Tracy told Stinger that he had one more chance, and that if he stepped out of line, she'd leave."

"I can't see how that would matter to a stickman like him."

"I hate that term. Stickman. It's so, I don't know, *guy*, you know? Like it's some big admirable deal to screw around with lots of women."

"Sorry."

"It's okay," I said, yawning. "I'm just being grumpy. I'm tired. I'll sleep on all of this. Thanks for your help."

"I'm not sure what help I've been. But keep dig-ging. You're going at it the right way, given the re-sources you've got at hand. But I've got some advice for you, if you'll take it."

"Of course," I said.

"First, put personal feelings aside. Don't let the fact that Barwell is a creep, and I agree that he is, by the way, make you see things that aren't there.

"I think, too, that you should add Avila to your list of suspects. He could have done it. He's the most obvious, remember, which is why he was arrested."

"I guess you're right," I admitted.

"What do you really know about him? Just the word of people you like. You must have learned by now that likable people can still do horrible things. That's what I mean about Barwell. You're ready to think the worst of him because he's not your type of person. Or of Stinger Swain and the janitor. Make sure the facts fit."

"Okay. Is that it?"

"No. One more thing. Promise me that you won't be alone with any of these guys. No one-on-one confrontations or meetings in dark alleys. I'm not around to ride to the rescue this time. And I'd rather you were alive than right, if you know what I mean."

"Yes, sir. I'm playing it super-cautious."

"End of lecture. I don't like it, but I know why you want to do it. So just be careful."

"I promise."

"And now it's time for Elwy and me to go to bed. We both miss you."

"At least you've got each other," I said.

"That's your opinion. I tolerate this beast sleeping with me, Kate. I don't consider him fit company."

"Don't let him hear you saying that."

"He's dead to the world. So will I be thirty seconds after I hang up this phone. I love you and miss you."

"Me too."

"One more thing. Can you get to the medical examiner?"

"If I can't, maybe Esther can. Why?"

"It would be interesting to know if she had sex before she died, for one thing."

"I'll get on it first thing," I said.

We talked for a few more minutes, just inconsequential stuff to put off having to say goodbye.

When I hung up, I cursed my job, put out the light, and went into a deep, exhausted, lonely sleep.

CHAPTER

28

Esther Hirsch told me she would be happy to check with Jennifer Wilson, the medical examiner.

"She's a friend," she said. "I'll be able to get it out of her. I would get it from the cops eventually anyway. Jen will just give me a sneak preview."

"Great. Tell me about it tonight."

"Seven o'clock."

"Can I bring anything?"

"Just your appetite."

"I can't wait," I said.

Then I called June Hoving. She agreed to meet at 11:00 and gave me directions to her house. It was in a part of town I didn't know, on a side street parallel to Highway 19, the Gulf Coast's main drag.

I missed the turn the first time and had to double back through the parking lot of a strip mall, built around the A-1 Veteran's Buy and Sell Gun Shop and Practice Range: "We Aim to Please." The bar next door was called Shooters. Really.

I was a bit early, so I pulled up and parked in front of the barred front door. I rang the bell and looked in. A large man came out from behind the stock shelves, looked me over, and buzzed me in from behind the counter.

"Good morning," he said, cheerfully. "How can we help you today?"

Korea was his war, if indeed he was a vet. He was in late middle-age, sturdy, but fit-looking, with a grey crew-cut and quite a bit of healthy pink scalp showing through.

"Can I show you something in a lady's pistol?" he asked.

I looked around at the cases and racks filled with more kinds of guns than I ever imagined existed. The cases were well-polished oak and sparkling glass. It had the reassuring look of an old-fashioned drugstore, and he the genial pharmacist, except for the instruments of death.

"Is this your store?"

"It is, indeedy, ma'am," he said, sticking out his manicured hand. "Captain Harold T. Marshall, U.S. Army, retired, at your service."

"You have a very nice shop," I said. "But I'm not buying today. I'm just looking for a bit of information."

"I surely hope I can help you," he said.

"You see, I'm from Canada," I said.

"Lovely country," he said. "The wife and I were up there a few years ago. My goodness, it's clean. Only they wouldn't let me bring my guns across the border. I had to double back and leave them with my daughter in Buffalo."

"Where did you visit?"

"Niagara Falls, first. We were there on our honeymoon, too, almost thirty-seven years ago now, just before I went overseas. It's changed a lot since then, though. Not as nice, in my opinion."

"Few things are," I said.

"You're right on the money there. Then we went to Stratford. My wife likes the plays. Next we went to a fishing camp up north aways and back down to Toronto to see our Titans play. We call 'em our Titans, too, don't you know. We feel like they're just home-town boys. Where are you from?"

"Toronto," I admitted. "In fact, that's my job, writing about the Titans."

"You don't say? You're one of them women who go into the locker room and all?"

"Well, yes, that's one part of my job."

"It's a pleasure to make your acquaintance," he said, shaking my hand again. "I have to tell you, I didn't think it was proper when I first heard about it, but my wife and my daughter set me straight pretty quick."

He laughed, and shook his head.

"They sure did set me straight," he said.

"I'm glad," I said.

"Well, I can't wait to tell my wife I met you," he said.

"Captain Marshall," I began.

"Oh, excuse me. I'm so sorry. You had something to ask me, didn't you. Of course you did."

"Just a couple of questions."

"Shoot," he said, looking pleased with himself. "Get it? Shoot!"

"That's a good one, Captain."

"Always gets a laugh," he chuckled.

"Can anybody buy a handgun in Florida?"

"Any Florida resident who is not a convicted felon or a person who has been institutionalized for mental illness is eligible to purchase firearms," he recited.

"Being from Canada, where, as you know, handguns are pretty closely controlled . . ."

He nodded, looking sad.

"I don't know much about them," I continued. "Is a .38 revolver a popular model?"

He went to a case, unlocked it, and took out a gun.

"This is your Smith and Wesson .38-calibre revolver," he said. "The basic model, the Police Special."

I accepted it gingerly. I'd seen one like it before, on the shelf in the hall closet where Andy leaves his when he gets home, but I had never touched it. It weighed a couple of pounds, and was an ugly, menacing, blue-black colour, with a wooden handgrip. It gave me the creeps.

"This is the gun used by the Sunland Police Department and other law enforcement agencies throughout North America," Marshall said. "I do believe the Toronto police force uses this gun."

"Right again. Why is that?"

"It's reliable," he said. "Its effectiveness lies in that your Smith and Wesson .38 can really stop a human being."

I put the gun down.

"What about for other people? Is it a popular gun with civilians?"

"It depends. Other guns are a bit flashier and fancier, they go in and out of fashion like clothes.

Those would be your automatics, Berettas and such. Every time a new spy movie comes out, we get a run on whatever guns are in it. But the Police Special sells well year-in and year-out. It's timeless."

Like a good tweed suit, I thought, or the basic black cocktail dress.

"Now, that's the standard gun, with the four-inch barrel. There are more deluxe models, of course. There, in the case, it's the same gun, but it has the chrome finish and the eight-inch barrel. It's accurate, but a bit showy, and definitely too much gun for a woman, if you don't mind my saying so."

"Looks like something I had with caps in it when I was a kid," I said. "How do you tell the standard guns apart? Where is the serial number?"

He picked the gun up and turned it over to show me the letters and numbers stamped into the bottom of the butt.

"And if you don't want it to be traced, you file that off, right?"

"That's what you see on most of your illegal guns, yes."

"What about those? Illegal guns?" I asked. "Are they hard to come by around here?"

"I wouldn't know anything about that," he said, all business, the sparkle gone.

"What if someone who wasn't a resident needed a pistol?"

"He couldn't buy it here."

"Where would he go?"

"Well, he could buy it privately, I suppose. There's nothing illegal about that. He might pick one up at a swap meet."

"A swap meet?"

"Sure, or a garage sale. No problem there. Are you sure you're not interested?"

"No, guns scare me," I said.

"You shouldn't be scared of guns," he said. "It's not the guns, it's the people using them you got to worry about."

"Of course," I said. "I really appreciate your help, Captain. It has been very interesting talking to you."

"Any time, little lady," he said. "And you take care of those Titans, you hear? You know, some of them are personal friends of mine."

"Really?"

"Why, sure. They come in here, and I'm able to help them out a bit, give them a little break on the price."

He gestured to a wall of photos I hadn't noticed before. I went closer to inspect them. There he was, Captain Harold T. Marshall, retired, shaking hands with Red O'Brien, the former manager; riding a golf-cart with Stinger Swain; posing at the ballpark with Joe Kelsey and Tiny Washington; deep-sea fishing with Archie Griffin and Flakey Patterson; even the late Steve Thorson was there, photographed with the captain at the target range. There were other ballplayers I recognized from other teams that train along the coast, and shots of Marshall posed with any number of dead animals to round off the hall of fame.

"Not that I've sold guns to all those fellows, mind you," he said.

"What about Stinger Swain?" I asked, pointing to his picture.

"He's been a customer," he said. "Of course, he's from Georgia, out-of-state, so I haven't been able to sell him a gun. But he has bought ammunition, and uses the range sometimes, him and the missus. He's quite the hunter, you know."

"I'd heard that," I said. "A lot of them seem to be."

"Well, it's relaxing," he said. "And peaceful. These ballplayers need that after the season is over, getting away from the stress and all."

"I guess so," I said, dubious. "I always wonder why they don't just go back to their families. I would think they would miss that."

"Well, family life can take some getting used to after the season, too, I guess," he said. "In some cases it's probably better that the husband goes away for a week or two."

"You could be right, Captain," I said. "Thanks again for all your help."

"My pleasure, Miss," he said. "Call in any time."

Fat chance of that, I thought, sweet as he was.

CHAPTER

29

June Hoving's street was small and cramped. There were no sidewalks, and the lawns, such as they were, were a far cry from the putting greens in more affluent parts of town. The cars in the driveways were junkers, not Cadillacs, some of them up on blocks. But it was livelier, and more friendly. You could tell people really lived there. A bunch of kids were horsing around with their bicycles on a lawn. At another house, a woman was working in the garden, which had one of those wooden standup cut-outs of a bending-over bum in a polka-dot dress. It was tacky, maybe, but full of life.

I found the Hoving house without too much trouble. It looked tidy, but in need of paint. There was a small garden, and some flowering bushes, growing out of control. Back by the garage I saw a vintage Corvette, gleaming red and white. A pair of legs, wearing jeans and cowboy boots, stuck out from underneath the open passenger door. Ringo, the mechanic, I assumed.

June was at the door when I got there. She looked more comfortable than the last two times I had seen her, dressed in jeans and a tie-dyed tee-shirt. Her hair was loose and freshly washed, thick and curly like Lucy's, but with quite a bit of grey. She looked younger and more attractive in casual clothes.

I followed her into the house. She seemed nervous.

"My husband's not here," she said. "I'm not sure if you wanted to talk to him, too."

"That's fine," I said. Even though I wanted another look at him after hearing Hank's story, I knew I would get more out of June without an audience.

"Can I get you something? I've just made a fresh pot of coffee."

"That would be lovely," I said.

When she went to the kitchen, I looked around the living room, a clean, comfortable place dominated by a large television set in one corner. The couch was covered with the kind of Indian-cotton pattern bedspread I hadn't seen since the late sixties. There were also large cushions on the floor, covered with the same stuff. The walls were painted deep red, and hung with framed posters. It was a cheery room, and reminded me of places I had lived as a university student. The smell did, too, sandalwood incense not quite masking the marijuana.

June came back into the room, carrying a tray with two pottery mugs of coffee and a matching sugar bowl and cream jug. She put the tray on the round brass table between a pair of armchairs by the window. We sat and busied ourselves with doctoring our coffees, then I put my tape recorder on the table.

"I hope you don't mind," I said. "It saves me having to take notes. And it prevents me from misquoting you."

"That's fine," she said, though she looked dubious.

"Did Lucy live here?" I asked.

"No, she moved out a few years ago, into an apartment behind the new mall," she said.

"How often did you see her?"

"A lot," she said. "She would come by here or I'd go over there or she'd drop into the restaurant. We were very close."

"Why did she move out?"

"She wanted her independence."

"There were no problems, then?"

"Well, she and Dirk really didn't get along that well," June said. "Don't be writing that, though. We just decided it would be better for everyone if she was on her own."

"You kept up with what she was doing, though."

"We didn't have any secrets from each other."

"Just from your husband."

"Well, yes," she said.

I waited for her to go on. Silence is sometimes more effective than a question. Finally, she sighed.

"Dirk is a good man, a good husband. But he was never a father before. Lucy and Ringo and I had been alone for a long time before I met Dirk, and we had our own ways. I trust them both. Lucy was no angel, but she was responsible. I figured that she could make up her own mind. Dirk couldn't accept that.

He laid down a lot of rules that she wouldn't follow. He treated her like a child, and she couldn't stand that."

"He was too rigid," I said.

"Exactly. He expected too much of her. It was pretty awful before she moved out. I hated the day she left, but I also realized it was for the best. Things have been better since then. Yeah, Dirk's a bit rigid, but I can live with it. I don't mind. I prefer a more settled life now, to tell the truth. Besides, he travels a lot, so I can do what I like."

"He's a trucker?"

"Yes, long-distance hauler. That's where he is now. Another one of the drivers called in sick, so he had to take a rig up to Detroit. He'll be gone a few days."

"Couldn't he have found someone else? You shouldn't be left alone right now."

"I don't mind, really. I prefer it, if you want to know the truth. There's been too much praying going on around here for the last few days. I've had to beat off the well-meaning church people with a stick."

"He is a religious man, I understand," I said.

"Born-again five years ago, now," she said.

"And you?"

"I went through the deal for him, because it meant a lot, but I don't take it too seriously. I figure it's what Dirk needs to keep himself under control. It has been a big help in his life, and that's good. As for me, I don't really need it."

"What about Ringo?"

"What about him? You mean is he born-again? No. He works for Dirk's trucking company. You know about that, right? Trucking for Jesus. Kind of embarrassing, if you ask me. Anyway, Ringo just works there."

"What about his relationship with his step-father?"

"Dirk was never as tough on him, I guess because he's a boy. A man. Dirk has different standards for men and women. Besides, Ringo isn't like Lucy. He just likes working on cars and hanging around with the guys."

"Your former husband told me he saw quite a bit of Lucy in recent years," I said. "Did you know about that?"

She looked very surprised.

"Hank Cartwright? No, I didn't know that. She never told me. Are you sure?"

"That's what he said. She saw him once a week."

"I never knew."

"Does it bother you?"

"Well, yeah. Geez. I mean it bothers me that she never told me. Why did she think she had to keep it a secret? I wouldn't have minded. Hank's okay, just a bit pathetic."

She laughed.

"Can you turn that thing off? I'd just like to talk a bit, not for the interview. Do you mind?"

I switched off the tape recorder.

"I don't have a lot of women friends," she explained. "Just people at work, and I don't like to talk to them about personal stuff."

"I understand that," I said.

"What's funny about her seeing Hank is that she isn't his daughter," she said.

It was my turn to be surprised.

"Of course, she didn't know that. Neither did he, and I wasn't going to tell either of them. So if she was looking for her father, she was looking in the wrong place. Funny, huh?"

"Does her real father know?"

"That he's her father? I never told him. Maybe he suspects," she shrugged. "I never saw any reason to tell him. I didn't expect him to do anything about it. I wanted to be with Hank back then anyway. Lucy was just a one-night mistake."

"You're sure about this."

"Oh, yeah. I knew when it was I got pregnant, and Hank wasn't around right then. He was out west for a month."

We both lit cigarettes.

"I realized I was pregnant after he got back. It was close enough that it could have been his, within a couple of weeks. So I just let him think it was."

"That's understandable, if you wanted to be with him."

"Those were different times. We were all stoned all the time. Sex was no big deal. We weren't into fidelity."

"Sex, drugs, rock and roll, and living for the moment," I said. "Be here now."

"You got it," she laughed. "I guess Lucy took after me. Promiscuity runs in the family. She did not give a flying fuck, excuse me, what other people thought. I was just like her at that age. Except Lucy was smart enough not to get pregnant. The Pill was harder to get back then. You're about my age, right? Remember? You had to get your parents' permission then, and there was no way I could ask my mom that. But Lucy? Hell, as soon as she began to date, I went and got her her own prescription."

"I remember those days too," I said. "Major anxiety, once a month."

"Fun, wasn't it?"

We laughed together.

"But we were lucky on one thing," she said. "The worst thing we could catch was a dose of the clap."

"I know. I'm glad I'm not a teenager these days. Or a parent of one."

"Lucy and I used to talk about safe sex all the time," she said. "Not that it did any good. She got herpes anyway. Said she forgot, or they didn't have any condoms, or the guy liked it better without."

"Of course, because they know they're invincible. Bad things happen to other people."

Suddenly she began to cry.

"Shit," she said. "It's just so damn unfair."

I watched her pain and cursed myself.

"I'm sorry," I said.

"Not your fault," she said. She got up and left the room, but came back a moment later with a fistful of tissues.

"I should put a box of these in every room these days," she said, then wiped her eyes and blew her nose. "Every time I think about her, I just start to bawl."

"It's not surprising," I said, feeling useless. "It's going to take a while."

"I don't think I'll ever get over it. Lucy was everything to me. I don't know how I will live without her."

She looked at me quickly.

"Don't get me wrong," she said. "I'm not going to do anything drastic. I'm a survivor. But I don't expect any happiness in my future."

The side door banged, and Ringo stood in the doorway, greasy from his work.

"Mom? You all right?"

"Fine, Ringo. Everything is fine."

"I'm going over to Bud's for a while, okay?"

"Yes. Just call if you're going to miss dinner."

"I'll be back before then," he said, then disappeared towards the back of the house. We could hear him going to the bathroom. She rolled her eyes at me, and we both laughed.

"Close the damn door," she yelled. "We've got company."

Sound of door closing, muffled apology, followed by a flush. Two minutes later, he was out the door.

She blew her nose again, then looked at me.

"I need a beer. Will you have one with me?"

"I wouldn't say no."

"Good. Bring your stuff into the kitchen."

CHAPTER

30

We sat at a round oak table by a window overlooking the tiny backyard, framed by hanging plants dangling in macramé. She carried some breakfast dishes to the sink, wiped the table with a dishcloth, and got two cans of beer out of the fridge. Its door was covered with a clutter of postcards, cartoons, and, I noticed sadly, some snapshots of Lucy.

"It's better in here," she said. "You want a glass?"

"Can's fine. I prefer kitchens, too."

"Let's get back to the interview, then. Turn on the damn machine and ask me your questions."

"Tell me about Lucy when she was younger," I said, setting up the tape recorder. "What was she like as a kid?"

"Same as she was when she grew up," she said. "Full of mischief. Determined. Once she set her mind on something you couldn't turn her around, no matter what.

"I remember she wanted a dog when she was

little. I wouldn't let her because I'm allergic. But she kept after me every day. She said she'd keep it out of doors, never let it in the house, never forget to feed it, and so on. She just had to have a pet. So, finally I gave in a little and got her a gerbil. But she didn't just cuddle it and watch it in its cage. Not Lucy. She called it Rin Tin Tin and trained it to walk on a leash."

I laughed with her.

"No kidding," she said. "It was the craziest damn thing. Every night after supper, she'd take it for a walk, just like a dog. I can still see her, eleven years old, setting out with that little furball on a leash. People laughed at her, but she didn't care. And the first thing she did when she left home was get herself that dog she'd always wanted. Did you ever see it? A beautiful German shepherd, just like Rin Tin Tin. She called him Gerbil. He went everywhere with her."

"I don't remember seeing him."

"He got killed by a car six months later. You know the saying, 'If I didn't have any bad luck, I'd have no luck at all'? That was Lucy, for a while. But she didn't let it get her down."

"What do you know about her relationship with Domingo Avila? Is there anything you know about them that might be a reason for him to, um, do what he is accused of doing?"

"Maybe he was jealous because she broke up with him, but I can't see why. They didn't go together very long. It started a couple of years ago in spring training, then again last year when he was playing with the Sunland minor-league team. He was just a kid. So was she, really, but he seemed younger. She was nice to him. She helped him with his English and taught him how to get along up here. She was kind that way."

"Was there bitterness about their breakup? Did he take it pretty hard?"

"I don't think there was any problem like that. He got called up to Knoxville and it was over. There was never anything serious between them. At least not on her side."

"I wonder if you are completely sure that he's the one who did it," I tried. She shrugged.

"Troy Barwell says the murder gun was found in the kid's apartment. He hasn't got an alibi. I guess the police know what they're doing. No, I'm not positive, but don't write that. We'll just have to wait for the trial. Besides, I don't really care, you know? Finding out who did it won't bring her back."

"But if Dommy's innocent he shouldn't be in jail. Whoever really did it should be there instead, don't you think?"

"I don't know. I just can't bring myself to give a shit right now. I don't feel like it's my problem. Can you understand that?"

"I guess so."

"Funny, because I can't," she said. "What else do you want to know?"

I looked at my notes.

"Aside from her pet, what did Lucy enjoy when she was young?"

"She always loved to write. I already told you that. She wrote stories and poems as soon as she could hold a pencil. She always got A's in English. She wasn't quite so good in math and science, but she was a top student."

"But didn't she win some county fair science project?"

"Yes. Tri-county fair. That was a long time ago. I'd almost forgotten. She did a genetics project breeding her gerbil. Rin Tin Tin turned out to be a girl. It was pretty crazy around here that year, I can tell you. It was only second prize, but we were real proud."

"Any other prizes or honours?"

"She was on part-scholarship at St. Petersburg Junior College. After she finished, she was going to go to journalism school up north. She was saving her money."

"Was she a joiner? Girl Scouts, that sort of thing?"

"Not really. She wasn't much for organized stuff. She was on the cheerleading squad, but that was so she could get with the athletes. I don't know where that came from, by the way. Certainly not from me. I never went out with jocks."

"Was there someone special? Did she go steady or give you any terrors about early marriage?"

"Not really. She usually went for the lost ones. I used to call them her stray dogs. There was one who is in a mental institution now, poor kid. Not through her doing. I think he would have been in there long before if it hadn't been for Lucy. But she couldn't be his nursemaid forever."

"This was the Bonder boy?"

"Yes. Arnie. How do you know about that?"

"Someone mentioned it. I can't remember who."

"Gossips," she said, shaking her head. "Everyone thinks our business is their business."

"This wasn't reported with any malice," I assured her.

"I know you don't mean any harm," she said. "But that was such a difficult time, with Arnie. It really broke her heart. She wasn't a cruel girl. Just the opposite. But no one understood."

"I guess his father is pretty bitter."

"Yes, he's the one. He's the only one. The boy didn't hate her. Just the father. You wouldn't believe the things he did. He sent her horrible letters and phoned her at all hours of the day and night. It just tore her apart."

"I guess it's pretty terrible to have that happen to your only son, though."

"Not as bad as what happened to my only daughter."

I reached across the table and took her hand and we sat in silence for a while. I was comfortable with June, strangely, and she seemed to be with me. After a moment, she got up and got two more beers. We lit cigarettes and looked out the window.

"Nice garden," I said.

"Thanks, I don't have time to do enough, but I like to be in it, when it's not too hot."

"It must be nice to be able to grow things all year round," I said. "I have a little garden, too, but last I heard it was covered in snow."

June shuddered.

"I've never seen snow," she said. "Except once, when we had a storm here five years ago. How can you can stand it?"

"To tell you the truth, I can't, but I manage, every year. We don't get a lot of snow in Toronto, anyway."

"But the cold. You can have it."

"Yeah, I'm stuck with it. Don't worry, I don't go out in it unless I absolutely have to. And you notice

I'm not completely dumb. I've found a job that brings me here every March."

She laughed.

"What are you going to do now?" I asked. "Will you go back to work?"

"Next week, probably. I can't see how hanging around the house is going to help me any. And the gang at work is pretty nice. Plus, we need the money."

"Is there any place here you can go for help? Anyone you can talk to?"

"A shrink, you mean?" she looked at me sharply. "I've had enough of them to last me a lifetime. When I was a kid."

"I didn't mean a shrink, necessarily. Maybe a Family of Victims group or a grief counsellor. Maybe a women's group. Just someone to talk to when you're feeling lost, somone who will understand. Do you have family that could help?"

"I was an only child, and my parents' car got T-boned on Highway 19 five years ago by some drunk in a pickup truck. They both died. So I guess I'm on my own."

She drained her beer.

"But it won't be the first time, and it probably won't be the last."

Another silence.

"Sorry," she said. "I know you mean well. But, like I told you, I'm a survivor. I'll be fine. Not happy, maybe, but I'll be fine."

She stood up.

"Now, if you'll excuse me, I think I'd like to be alone for a while."

I apologized and gathered up my things.

"One more thing," I said, hating to drag the words out. "Could I borrow a picture of Lucy, for the article? I'd get it back to you."

She turned, without a word, and came back with a colour photo in a silver frame, a head and shoulder shot of Lucy, smiling mischievously.

"That's a really nice picture," I said.

"It's my favourite one," she said, with a catch in her voice. "You take good care of it."

I took it out of the frame and handed the frame back.

"I'll return this tomorrow or the next day," I said. "Also, the paper wants our photographer to take some pictures of you and Ringo, maybe. Would you be willing?"

She looked blankly at me.

"I don't mind, but I don't know when he's getting back."

"Not today, necessarily. I'll call you later in the afternoon and we can set it up, okay?"

"Fine," she said, and walked me to the door. On an impulse, I hugged her. She hugged me back.

"I'll call and see how you're doing," I said. "Maybe we'll get together."

"I'd like that," she said. "I really would."

When I got into my car, which was parked three or four houses away, I caught sight of another car in my rear-view mirror, turning into her driveway. Curious, I waited before starting the car, long enough to see Cal Jagger walk up to her front door and ring the bell.

CHAPTER

31

I didn't feel like going back to the hotel to write. It was too nice a day. I'd be spending the first few hours staring at my screen and waiting for inspiration anyway. I could do that just as well in the sunshine. Besides, I hadn't seen any baseball for close to a week. I headed to the training complex. If I was lucky, there would even be some lunch left.

The players were heading back out to the practice fields when I got there. I went into the media room and made myself a couple of sandwiches and took them out to the stands behind home plate. I was alone, mercifully. The fans aren't allowed inside until the exhibition season starts, and the rest of the reporters were off doing other things. Trying to find something new to write about, no doubt. Poor buggers.

So it was just me and the sunshine, and the sights, sounds, and smells of the game I love. The strong young men hitting and running and fielding and throwing against the green of the grass and blue of the sky; the chatter around the batting cage, shouted insults and laughter, calls of encouragement, the sweet crack of bat on ball; the air flavoured with red-clay dust, a hint of pine tar, and traces in olfactory memory of last season's hot dogs and popcorn.

Horkins Field, or more correctly, the Dwight G. Horkins baseball complex, was named after the former mayor of Sunland who convinced the Titans that his little corner of paradise was just what they needed for their spring-training camp.

The stadium proper, which is surrounded by practice fields, had originally been the town's high-school showcase, and still has a cosy, amateur feeling to it, despite the money the town and the Titans have spent upgrading it. The field itself is in great shape, but the stands, at field level only from foul pole to foul pole, still feel like bleachers. The right-field seating is on benches with lines painted on them to delineate assigned places, and on busy afternoons the public address announcer asks patrons to "smoosh over so we can fit a few more folks in."

The outfield fences are painted with advertisements for local businesses: among them the Hiram Wesley Insurance Company, the Bicentennial Savings and Loan, The El Rancho Roadhouse, the All-Globe Travel Agency, Betty's Dress Shoppe ("Gently Used Clothing for the Fuller Figure"), the good old A-1 Veteran's Buy and Sell Gun Shop and Practice Range, and, in deepest centre field, Morley the Jeweler, who offers a diamond ring to the lucky player who hits a home run through a circle about ten inches in diameter. At last report, Morley hadn't yet had to part with any of the merchandise. All the signs, although newly painted, had a fifties feeling to them. But then, so does baseball.

During the summer, the stadium is the home of the rookie-league Titans, at the low end of the minor-league ladder. The practice fields are used by little-league, school, and other amateur community teams. It is a good deal for everyone, even though both sides grumble every year during contract renewal.

I slumped happily with my feet on the seat in front of me, enjoying the moment totally. There were six players involved in the current round of batting practice with Sugar Jenkins, the batting coach: Stinger Swain, Kid Cooper, David Sloane, Eddie Carter, Joe Kelsey, and Jack Asher.

They were playing a game Asher brought with him from the Padres, his former team. It was a variation of the simulated games most teams play during batting practice. The Padres variation involved demerits as well as points awarded for each type of hit. The outfielders were competing against the infielders, with Asher qualifying for the second team by virtue of being a terrible first baseman before he moved to the American League and hung up his glove for good.

There was an extra edge to the competition, because they were facing what they call live pitching. Instead of the usual coach serving up soft tosses, the hitters were facing Bony Costello, the left-handed ace of the Titan staff. He wasn't exactly in mid-season form, but he was hard to hit nevertheless.

They were having fun, something they forget to do sometimes in the heat of the season. They could have been kids in the schoolyard instead of the multinational sport conglomerates they really are. I was having fun watching them, too, which is something I also forget from time to time under the pressure of deadlines and scrambling for scoops.

When Costello was done, Flakey Patterson took his place on the mound. There were loud protests from the hitters, who wanted to face a right-hander this time. After a few pitches, they were howling. Patterson was trying out his large repertoire of junk pitches, knuckle balls, and tantalizing floaters. The hitters couldn't touch them.

"Stop throwing shit," Swain yelled. His team was behind in the make-believe game. "Pitch like a man, not a pussy."

Flakey floated another one in. Swain swung mightily and missed.

"What do you call that swing, Stinger?" asked Eddie Carter.

"A pussy swing," said Patterson. "You ready for a fastball?"

Swain stood in and swung his bat back and forth slowly, finally pointing it into centre field. Patterson wound up and threw the fastball, high and inside. Swain ended up in the dirt, to general hilarity all around. Even Sugar Jenkins joined in.

"They better not let the skipper catch them having fun," said Tiny Washington, dropping into the seat two away from mine. "He'll fine their asses."

"For having fun?"

"Not allowed in this camp."

"I guess you retired just in time," I said.

"Guess I did," he said, taking the lid off a styrofoam coffee cup.

"Do you miss it?"

He looked at the players around the batting cage.

"I'd be lying if I said I didn't."

"You'll get used to it."

"That's what I'm afraid of," he said. "Maybe I should have got right out of the game, so I wouldn't have to be around it all the time."

"What would you do?"

"Spend some time with my family. Start a business. My brother wants to open a restaurant with me back home."

"Tiny, you'd go nuts without baseball. Besides, you're going to be a good broadcaster."

He shrugged and drank his coffee. I'd never seen him so down.

"Wow, it's like a big black cloud just moved in," I said.

"Two out of three ain't bad," he said.

"What?"

"I'm not a cloud."

That lightened the mood a bit.

"Have you been doing any talking to the players about the night Lucy was shot?"

"A little. I found out what Stinger got so hot at Lucy for."

"Really?"

"She was asking Tracy about the baby, remember? Well, it was last spring training she had that baby, and that's when Stinger and Lucy were getting it on."

"Which is why she remembered so clearly when it was born."

"Uh huh. And there's more. The same time Tracy got the baby, Stinger got something else."

217

"This wouldn't be a social disease that starts with the letter H, would it?"

"You got it."

"No, as a matter a fact, I haven't," I said.

"But Stinger does, and so does Mrs. Stinger, and she wasn't too happy about it."

"You would think Stinger would know better. Condoms aren't exactly a new invention. But he's probably one of those guys who thinks real men don't wear them."

"That's all changed now," Tiny said.

"Did you find out anything else?"

"Not really. What have you heard about Dommy?"

"I'm seeing his lawyer tonight. Maybe she'll have some news. She says he's okay."

"Hope so," Tiny said. "I hate to think about him in that jail."

"Me, too. But they got him taken out of the general population into some sort of protective custody."

"What time is it?"

I looked at my watch.

"Two-thirty."

"I'm interviewing Olliphant at three. Big deal thing for the weekend special. Got any ideas?"

"You want me to do your job for you?"

"Come on, Kate. This is all new to me. I never know what questions to ask."

"Well, you could take it position by position and ask him to evaluate the team. You could ask him which rookies are looking good so far. You could ask him about his starting rotation for the Grapefruit League next week."

"Don't go so fast," Tiny said. He was writing it all down.

"Ask him about the American League, how long it's going to take him to catch up on it, what he's doing to learn the players on the other teams."

"Good, good."

"You could ask him why he never holds a job for more than a couple of years. Is it because he's a pig-headed jerk."

"Yeah, sure."

"I just said you could ask him, not that you should ask him."

"You're trying to get me in trouble, woman."

"You're lucky you were always nice to me all those years you were playing. I wouldn't do this for just any rookie."

"Well, I'm much obliged," he said, heaving his bulk out of the seat. "Now I'd better go get ready."

"Don't forget to powder your nose."

He grunted ruefully and left. I decided my holiday was over, too. I wanted to get a start on the Lucy piece before I went to Esther's for dinner.

I went down the aisle and climbed over the barrier between the stands and the field. Gloves waved at me from the batting cage, so I went over.

"Were you telling Tiny any news?" he asked.

"Nothing too interesting," I said. "Have you got anything?"

He looked at Stinger, who was on the other side of the cage, staring at us. When I caught his eye, he looked quickly away.

"Not that I want to talk about now," Gloves said. "I think Karin's been asking around about some things. Maybe you should call her."

"I'll do that as soon as I get home. Thanks. Who's winning?"

"Outfielders," he said. But we'll get to them once Flakey's out of there."

He turned and shouted towards the mound.

"Hey, Flakey. You don't want to be overdoing it now. You don't want to blow out your shoulder before the exhibition season starts."

"Man, if the other teams' hitters are as lame as you guys, I'm gonna get me a Cy Young this year," he answered. His cap sat strangely on his head, which was covered with fine stubble.

"You win anything, it's going to be the Cy Old," said Eddie Carter, who was at bat. "You pitch like my Grandpa."

"Who's your Grandpaw, Satchel Paige?" Flakey hollered back.

There was only one player not laughing. Stinger Swain hadn't even been listening. He was looking at me with icy hatred in his eyes, swinging his bat towards me. I got out of there.

CHAPTER

32

I put on the kettle when I got home and called Karin. She sounded harried when she answered the phone, and there was the sound of a baby screaming in the background.

"I'm babysitting," she explained. "I've got Justin and Ashley. He just bopped her on the head with a ninja stick. Let me just go try and straighten it out."

I held, listening to the sound of Karin simultaneously soothing the little girl and laying down the law to her brother. The crying stopped, but the whining didn't. Then I heard the sound of the television playing cartoons.

"I don't let my kids watch in the afternoon, but that's what these two are used to," she said, a little defensively, once she came back to the phone.

"Where is their mother?"

"She's at some church thing, then getting her hair done."

"So you got to be the lucky one."

"Yeah, but now she owes me."

"Big, from the sound of it."

"She doesn't know how big."

"Gloves said you'd been asking some questions around the complex," I said. "Did you find out anything that might help Dommy at all?"

"Not really. I've been trying to figure out how that gun got switched, but I can't find out who was alone in Alex and Dommy's place that night. The super was in on Saturday, but that was legitimate. He was repairing a cupboard door that got broken Friday night."

"A legitimate reason, maybe, but that doesn't mean he didn't do something else while he was there."

"No, except that someone would have seen him carrying the gun."

"Not necessarily. Doesn't he carry a toolbox?"

"Well, yeah. But how would he know on Friday night that he would be able to make the switch?"

"True."

"And I found someone else who was awake when Goober was throwing up in the garden."

"Who?

"Clarice Carter. And she remembers the time. It was quarter of two."

"So that's about half an hour before the murder. Did Clarice see anything else?"

"She says Goober went into his place then. She also says there was a light on at Alex and Dommy's place when she looked out and saw Goober. When she looked again five minutes later it was off."

"Did she see anybody leaving the apartment?"

"No, just the light going out."

"Do you have her number?"

"She's just outside. Do you want me to get her?"

"Thanks."

A few minutes later, Clarice was on the line with her breathless, little-girl voice. She couldn't add anything to what Karin had already told me.

"I didn't see anything else. Just the light go off. What do you think it means?"

"If Lucy was with Dommy that night, it could be that's when she left. But you're sure you didn't see anyone else, or hear anything? A car or something?"

"No. There was nothing."

"Was it quiet?"

"Yes. I heard a baby crying, but that was later."

"How much later?"

"I was almost asleep again. I didn't see the time. But it was maybe fifteen minutes?"

"Could you tell were it was coming from?"

"No, but there are only a few families with babies in the complex. The Ashers, the Sloanes, and the Swains."

"How long did the crying go on?"

"A long time, it seemed like. I wondered about that. But I guess I fell asleep."

"That's interesting."

"What do you think it means?"

"I don't know yet, but it might be important."

"I hope it helps."

"Me too," I said. "I've got to go now. Thanks a lot."

The kettle was boiling ferociously. I made a pot of tea, poured a mug, and took it back to my desk. I plugged in my tape recorder and began to transcribe the relevant parts of my interview with June Hoving.

It took a couple of hours. It's the most tedious

part of my job, and I hate it. Some reporters use tape recorders all the time, but I avoid them except for difficult interviews like the one I did with June, when scribbling notes can be threatening and destroy rapport. Athletes are used to talking to people who are looking at their notepads, but normal people need to feel like they are having a conversation.

Anyway, as usual, I winced listening to my stupid questions, and transcribed more than I could possibly use in my story. The part of my mind that wasn't engaged in the boring process was working over the information I'd learned in the past few days.

I thought I had known Lucy before she was killed. I was wrong. I didn't know anything of her talent, her aspirations, or the battles she had fought and won. I hadn't liked her or given her any of the respect she was due. I had been as blinded as any sexist jerk by the Lucy on the surface; her clothes, her hair, her fingernails.

I wished I had been nicer to her. I wished I'd even taken the time to read something she had written. I probably would have liked it. I should have listened to her when she was talking about helping each other. I should have heard that she was asking for my help.

I listened to her mother's voice on the tape, and to her tears. With a little less luck, I could have been her. I could have had a daughter Lucy's age. The child I decided not to have when I was in my final year at university would have been grown up by now.

I pushed the maudlin thoughts away and concentrated on the tape, transcribing the pain into careful notations in my lined steno-pad while questions marched around my brain.

Did Hank Cartwright know he wasn't Lucy's father? Did Lucy know? Was it Lucy turning out the light at Dommy's place that night? Where had she gone? Who had she met? Was she followed? What went wrong? Why did she die? Who hated her enough to kill her?

I hadn't found any answers by the time I had finished working, and the questions continued while I showered and changed to go to Esther's.

I had just closed the door when I heard the phone ring. I considered for a moment just ignoring it, but then unlocked the door and went back in.

At first, I thought the caller had hung up. I said hello a couple of times, irritated. Then I heard a muffled voice.

"Shut up and listen," he said. "I'm only going to warn you once. Back off or you're going to end up like Lucy. I know where you live. I know what kind of car you drive."

Then the line went dead.

CHAPTER

33

"Oh, my God," Esther said. "What did you do?"

"Nothing," I said. "I just got out of there."

"Why didn't you call the police?"

"Who? Troy Barwell?"

"God, this is awful," Esther said. "You're sure you didn't recognize the voice?"

"It sounded like he was disguising it. Or he had a towel over the receiver or something. It was just a whisper. It could even have been a woman. I checked with the desk and she said the call came from outside the hotel. The person had asked for me by room number, not by name."

"So he does know where you live."

"I guess so."

"Not anymore," Esther said, taking charge. "As of tonight, you're staying here until this thing is over. And you're going to ditch that car."

"I came over in a cab," I said.

"Good thinking. We'll rent you another one tomorrow. Different kind, different colour. Even better, you can use mine. I'll borrow my parents' second car."

"I can rent, don't be silly."

"Kate, my parents have three cars."

"Why?"

"Because they keep one for my sister to use when she comes to town for the holidays. Makes sense to them!"

We both laughed. It cut the tension. We were sitting on the balcony of Esther's place, on the eighth floor of an upscale waterfront condo a couple of towns up the coast from Sunland. The place was as formal as she was casual. The living room was large and tidy, with sea-green leather furniture and glass and brass tables. The art on the walls was modern and bold. There were potted plants by the sliding doors out to the balcony. We sat in pretty white wicker chairs, drinking a nice California Chardonnay and waiting for Cal. Her tortoiseshell cat sat on the ledge, watching the gulls, longingly.

"Doesn't that make you nervous?" I asked, indicating her precariously poised pet.

"She hasn't fallen yet. She's a climber. Always has been, always will, I suspect. I don't think she really likes it on the ground."

As if aware that she was the centre of conversation, the cat looked at us, yawned, and began licking her bum.

"That's disgusting, Darrow," Esther said. " Where are your manners?"

"Cats have no manners," I said. "Besides, this is her house. She can do what she wants."

"Yes, I'm surprised she even tolerates us being here."

Having found common ground, we happily told stories about our respective felines for fifteen minutes until Cal arrived.

"Sorry to be late," he said. "Small family crisis."

"Nothing serious, I hope?"

"No. Sean was late back from school with the car. He needed a little fatherly lecture."

"Teenagers, gag," Esther said. "You'll never catch me with one of those around."

"Yes, but the little adorable ones you are so fond of have a bad habit of growing up," Cal said.

"Well, if I ever do find someone to father my children, I'll send them off to military academy from age twelve on."

"What about the girls?"

"What's wrong with military academy for girls? You a sexist or what?"

"Sean's a good kid," Cal said. "He just happens to be sixteen. He's better behaved than I was."

"From what I hear, a lot better behaved," Esther said. "And look how boring you grew up to be. So don't worry."

"Yes, counsellor," he said. "Got any beer?"

"Help yourself. You know where to find it."

He went to the kitchen, came back with a beer can, and pulled up another chair.

"I hope you didn't start without me," he said.

"We wouldn't dare," Esther said.

"Anyone know who did it yet?" he asked. "Any smoking guns or mysterious brown-paper envelopes?"

Esther told him about my threatening phone call. He was as alarmed as she had been. I tried to play it down, for my own sake as much as for theirs.

"The one thing is, maybe this means we're getting close," I said. "Or else he thinks we are. I wish I knew why. Every time I think I'm starting to see the solution, something else comes along to confuse me."

"Well, let's see what we've got, then," Cal said. "Maybe we know more than we think."

"First I want to hear about Dommy," I said. "Did you see him today, Esther?"

"Yeah, he's getting really depressed. And paranoid. He thinks he's never going to get out because he's a Dominican. That he's being framed because of it."

"That's not paranoid," Cal said. "It's probably true."

"When you talk with Dommy, do you speak in English or through an interpreter?" I asked.

"No, Spanish."

"Which she speaks fluently," Cal said.

"It's practically a prerequisite for practising criminal law in the state of Florida," she said.

"Did he have anything to say about the night of the murder?"

"He was embarrassed, but he says he was with Lucy. They had sex. That was at one or a little after, he said. He went to sleep and didn't wake up until the next morning."

"That fits with something I heard today," I said, and told them about the light in Dommy's apartment.

"He also was with her when Stinger flipped out," Esther said, "but he didn't know what it was about."

"I think maybe I do," I said, and told them Tiny's theory about Stinger and the present he had given Tracy after his liaison with Lucy.

229

"I guess that would be enough to do it," Cal said.

"Dommy also said that Axel Bonder, the super, was nosing around the apartment, his and Jones's, on Sunday afternoon," Esther said.

"What was he doing there?"

"Dommy doesn't know. He came back from the ballpark late and found Bonder on the patio, at the door. He said he was checking to make sure it was locked."

"Had Bonder been inside?"

"Dommy doesn't know. He felt like things were out of place, but he wasn't sure. Alex had been there earlier, but he'd gone out for dinner. And it was only a sense that things had been messed up."

"Karin told me that he was in there on Saturday, doing repairs to something." I said. "Maybe she got the day wrong."

"But we should ask Bonder about it, for sure," Cal said.

"There's more," Esther said. "Dommy also told me that his gun wasn't loaded. He didn't have any bullets for it yet. He can't understand how it could have been the murder weapon."

"Which makes sense of the theory that the murder gun was planted," Cal said.

"And he got it from Lucy?" I asked.

"Just before the party."

"Does he know where she got it?"

"No. He said she told him she could get him one if he wanted. He said sure. A couple of days later, she showed up at the condo with it. The afternoon of the party."

"Damn. I forgot to ask her mother if she knew about the gun when I was there this morning," I said.

230

"Did you get anything interesting from her?" Esther asked.

"I'm not sure if it's significant," I said. "I liked her, though. Did she tell you anything, Cal? I saw you arrive as I was leaving."

"No, she mainly talked about Lucy, and we chewed over some old times."

"Well, she told me something. It's juicy, but not necessarily relevant. It seems that Hank Cartwright wasn't Lucy's real father."

Cal looked uncomfortable.

"Did she tell you, too?" I asked.

"Yeah, as a matter of fact, she did," he said.

He took a drink. I waited, watching the sun sinking suddenly into the ocean. The cat jumped onto my lap.

"Well, what do you think?" Esther asked. "Do you think it has any bearing on the murder?"

"What the hell," Cal said. "I told Beth about it this afternoon. I was Lucy's father."

Esther and I looked at Cal, then at each other. He looked at the can of beer in his hands.

"Your family crisis wasn't about Sean and the car, then," she said, finally.

"No that was last week's. I substituted it. I'm not much of a liar, I guess."

He stopped and drank some beer.

"It was all so long ago," he said. "I was just a kid. "And she never told me until today. I was shocked. I should have known. I can't believe I didn't figure it out before."

"You showed up at a very vulnerable time," I said.

"There's been nothing between us since then," he said, looking at Esther, his wife's friend, who was looking coldly at him. "There wasn't much even then, just a brief time when Hank was out west."

"How do you feel about it?" I asked.

"Shocked, like I said. It's too much. To discover I had a daughter, and she's dead."

"Do you think she knew?"

"June says she never told her. But that's why she sent Lucy to get a job at the *Sentinel* with me. She wanted us to get to know each other."

"How is Beth?" Esther asked.

"She's all right, a bit shaken, but fine," he said. "Even though we were dating at the time it happened, she realizes that it had nothing to do with her, or that if it was a betrayal, it was another man betraying another woman in very different times. She is an extraordinary woman. I am very lucky that I came back and found her again."

"You bet your ass you are," Esther said, then got up, walked over to Cal, and gave him a fierce hug. That done, she stood, pushed up the sleeves of her sweater, and laughed a bit.

"All this drama makes me hungry," she said. "As what doesn't? I'm going to fix dinner."

"Can we help?" I asked.

"No, but you can come into the kitchen and talk to me while I work," she said.

CHAPTER

34

Esther's kitchen was small, but efficient. There was a frying pan simmering on the stove, sending out tantalizing smells of garlic. There was also a large pot of water at the boil on the back burner. Esther went to the fridge and took out salad and a big bowl full of littleneck clams in their shells.

"We're having Spaghetti alla Puttanesca," she said, with a broad attempt at an Italian accent. "With clams. I hope you like it."

"What can I do?" I asked.

"Are you any good at salad dressing?"

"It's probably my greatest strength in the kitchen," I admitted. "Some would say my only strength."

"You're on. The oil and vinegar and junk are in the cupboard next to the sink. Cal, your job is to set the table. You know where everything is."

We chatted inconsequentially as we worked, about anything but the two topics most on our

233

minds: murder and paternity. Ten minutes later, we were at her dining-room table serving ourselves spaghetti, perfectly sauced, with the clams just opening in their shells. The food was spicy with hot peppers, anchovies, and olives, and was absolutely delicious. Our only communication was grunts of pleasure until we had wiped up the last remnants of sauce with pieces of crusty bread.

"Coffee?" Esther asked, collecting our plates.

"Perfect," I said.

"I'll bring you an ashtray."

"If you don't mind," I said.

"I might even have one myself," she said, coming back in, with a tray of coffee things. "I indulge myself once in a while, especially after a good meal."

"Feel free," I said, pushing the pack towards her.

She took one and lit it, then settled back and smiled.

"Makes my head swim," she said. "And I love it."

"What the hell," said Cal, and reached for the pack.

"You're a terrible influence," Esther said.

"Just think of it as being a gracious hostess," I said. "It is so kind of you both to sacrifice your purity to make me feel comfortable."

"Right," Esther said. "Let me just get the coffee, and we'll get back to the problem at hand."

When she left the room, I looked at Cal. He had been quiet all evening, without any of his usual energy and humour.

"You okay?" I asked.

He rubbed his hands over his face.

"Not really," he said. "I guess I'm still a bit in shock. I feel really tired. Exhausted."

"That's no surprise," I said. "Do you want to go home? This isn't so important it can't wait."

"No, I want to stay. Today's, uh, newsflash, makes what we are doing more important than ever."

"You know, June told me that no one else knew, but I wonder," I said. "If Lucy found out, it might throw a whole new ingredient into the mix. If she told Hank, for example."

"That might screw his head around pretty good," Cal agreed. "But why would he want to kill her?"

"Hey, this isn't fair," Esther said, coming back into the room with a pot of coffee. "I'm being the serving wench and I'm missing all the good stuff."

"We're talking about Hank Cartwright," I said. "What if he knew he wasn't Lucy's dad?"

"Well, it certainly wouldn't make him want to kill her," she said.

"You're right," I said. "But still, I had the feeling there was something he wasn't telling me when I talked to him after the funeral. I missed something, somehow. Maybe something I should have picked up on, a question I should have asked. It's really bugging me."

"I think I'll go see him later tonight," Cal said.

"Not without me, you won't," I said.

"I guess it will be a threesome, kids, because I'm not staying home," said Esther.

"We can probably find him at that bar near the church," I said. "He seemed to be a regular."

"The fabulous Starlite? You're probably right," said Cal.

"Coffee first," Esther said. "I need fortification before taking that place on."

"Maybe if I see him again, I'll be able to figure

out what he was holding back," I said. "Something he wanted to tell me. I'd like to find out what it is."

"I'd just like a bit of action," Cal said. "All this speculating is making me twitch."

"But if he knows that you are Lucy's father, won't he freak out when he sees you?" Esther asked. "It might interfere. I think Kate and I should see him alone."

"Forget it," he said.

Esther and I exchanged a look. An exasperated, men-are-such-jerks-sometimes, kind of look.

"What, we little ladies need your protection going into a rough bar?" Esther asked.

"No, God damn it, I don't mean that," he said, angrily. "I just don't want to be left out of this."

"I understand how you feel," I said. "But you've told me yourself that he can get pretty crazy when he's drunk. I don't think he'll do that with me, but you might set him off."

"No. That's final. I'm in this all the way," he said.

The phone rang. Esther went to the kitchen to answer it. Cal and I looked at each other. He glared.

"You can't stop me," he said. "You have no right. I deserve to be there."

"Maybe you're right," I said. "Maybe you should be there for the conversation. But what if we went and got him out of the bar. It might avoid a scene."

Esther came back into the room.

"That was Jenny Wilson," she said. "The medical examiner. Lucy was: a) not pregnant, b) positive for herpes, and c) sexually active the night of her death. With two different men. There were traces of semen vaginally and orally. The former is probably Dommy's. The latter is unknown."

236

Cal looked pale and upset.

"Find the mystery man, and we've got the murderer," he said.

"You don't think it's Hank Cartwright?" Esther asked.

"I doubt it," I said. "Their relationship was a bit perverse, but I can't imagine them having sex on the beach. But that doesn't mean we shouldn't track him down and see if he's got anything else to tell us."

We went in Cal's suburban van, listening to a Beach Boys tape on Cal's stereo. *Pet Sounds*. The man has taste. It gave the outing a feeling of adventure and fun, and took the grimness out of our mission. It was also a bit surreal.

Cal pulled into the little lot and parked. I put my hand on his arm when he went to remove the keys.

"Please," I said. "Just wait here. We'll bring him right out. I promise."

He switched the ignition on again without saying a word, turned up the sound, leaned back against the headrest, and closed his eyes as music filled the car. The Beach Boys were singing "I just wasn't made for these times."

"Be careful," Cal said. "And if you're not back in ten minutes, I'm coming in."

"Okay, John Wayne, you got yourself a deal," Esther said. We jumped out of the van and crossed the parking lot. Motorcycles and pickup trucks again, but this time there were more of them.

Inside it was like a scene from a movie of the week about folks on the wrong side of town. The lighting was perfect, in smoky pools and shadows around the pool tables. The people were from Central Casting: tattooed bikers with beards and big bellies, mean black dudes in funny hats, acne-scarred women in tight pants and tank-tops, scrawny middle-aged white guys with squints. The music came from the jukebox. It wasn't the Beach Boys, and it drowned out the television, which was showing "L.A. Law." Anne Kelsey was in earnest conversation with Stewart Markowitz. No one in the bar but me seemed to care about their marital problems.

Cecil was in his usual spot at the bar, helped out at this hour by a tired-looking woman, perhaps his wife, who exchanged wisecracks with the customers.

Cecil saw us coming, and walked over to the empty end of the bar. We joined him, aware of the many eyes staring at us.

"Is Hank around?" I asked. Cecil couldn't hear me.

"Hank Cartwright," I shouted. "Have you seen him?"

Cecil pointed to a dark corner near the men's room. I could just make out Hank's slumped form in the gloom. He sat alone at a table, his back to the wall.

"Is he paid up?" I yelled. "We're taking him out of here."

"No problem," said Cecil.

"Thanks," I shouted. We crossed the room. The pool players, male and female, made a point of not getting out of our way, forcing us to brush past them, while they grinned like wolves. It didn't faze me. I had been through the same gauntlet in several visiting locker rooms. I looked at Esther. She had "don't mess with me" written all over her. There were no worries there.

We got to Hank's table. He was out of it, oblivious. I touched him on the shoulder. He started and glared at me. It took a moment for him to recognize me. When he did, tears filled his eyes. He spoke. I leaned closer.

"I killed her," he said. "I killed my little girl."

CHAPTER

35

"If you say so, Hank," I said loudly, directly into his left ear. "Why don't you come with us and tell us about it?"

We helped him from his chair, then led him out of the room. He stumbled a few times, but was steadier than I had feared he would be.

When we got to the car and opened the door, he saw Cal, and began to cry harder. He slumped in the passenger seat, sobbing.

"Cal, my old friend. My baby's gone," he said. "I killed my baby."

So much for the theory that he knew about Lucy's paternity. I looked at Cal. He was staring at Hank, astonished. So was Esther, who hadn't heard what Hank said to me in the bar. I shook my head at them.

"Cal, I think we should take Hank home and hear him out," I said. "Do you know where he lives?"

"You still behind Rita and Tom, Hank? Over on Cypress?"

Cartwright nodded his head. Esther and I jumped into the back. We rode through the empty streets, past block after block of tidy bungalows, lights all out, before turning right on Alternate Highway 19, the old shore road. The only sound was Hank Cartwright, snuffling and muttering. A mile or so farther, we turned up a street that quickly became a dirt road, past ramshackle houses and an autobody shop. There wasn't a cypress to be seen.

"Which house it it?" Cal asked. Hank indicated a driveway to the left, next to a house with the lights on and the sound of music and voices arguing inside. We got out. A dog barked.

"Shut up," Hank shouted, heading towards an old trailer up on blocks at the very back of the large untended yard.

We followed him, picking our way through weeds and garbage to the cinder blocks that served as his doorstep. Hank fished the key out from under a flower pot filled with dead plants, opened the door, and turned on the lights.

The place was surprisingly neat, if under-furnished. The fake wood-panelled walls were bare, and the floor was of shabby brown and white marble-patterned linoleum, worn through in spots. There was a two-seat booth with a table in it in the kitchen area, and a day-bed and rocking chair in the living room, which also had a stand with a small black and white television set on it, and brick-and-board bookshelves filling one wall. Half held books, the other half records and tapes. The stereo system ran along the top ledge. A hall led to what was probably the bedroom and bathroom area. I could see more book-cases through an open door.

Hank headed for the rocking chair, obviously his favourite place. There was a standing lamp beside it, and a shelf close to hand, with an ashtray, matches, and rolling papers.

Cal went to the day-bed and sat down. Esther went to the sink and filled a kettle.

"See what you can find in the way of coffee or tea," she told me. I looked through various canisters and found old cookies, baggies of drugs, and, finally, some ancient-looking tea bags of assorted sizes.

"It's probably herbal," I said, handing her the can.

"That's okay, as long as it's not alcoholic."

I sat next to Cal on the day-bed.

"Let's talk, Hank," I said. "Why do you say you killed Lucy? I don't think you pulled the trigger."

He wiped his nose on the sleeve of his sweat-shirt.

"I might as well have," he said.

"You got her the gun she gave Dommy. Domingo Avila," I guessed. "Is that what you mean?"

"I didn't know he was going to use it on her," he shouted. "I didn't know he was going to kill her!"

"He didn't, Hank," I said, gently. "Believe me, it had nothing to do with that gun."

Esther brought him a cup of tea. He looked at her for the first time.

"Who are you?"

"Esther Hirsch," she said. "I'm a lawyer."

I interrupted before she could tell him who her client was.

"She's a friend, Hank. You can trust her."

He put the mug down on the ledge next to him. "Anyone got a cigarette?" he asked.

I handed him one. He tore the filter off. I lit it.

"She's right, Hank," Cal said. "We think that it was another gun that killed Lucy. Her killer just planted it in Avila's apartment."

"Where did you get the gun, Hank?" I asked. He shrugged.

"Off a guy."

"The guy have a name?" Cal asked.

"Sonny, down at Cecil's place. Big guy. Beard."

"Where did he get it?" Esther asked.

"Didn't ask him," Hank said, sipping on his tea. He made a face and put it back down. "Stole it, probably. I heard him talking about it. Lucy asked if I knew where to get one, so I bought it off him."

"With whose money?" I asked.

"Lucy gave me a couple hundred bucks. That guy's money, I guess. Avila."

"What kind of a gun was it?"

"Police Special."

"Did it have a serial number?" I asked.

"No. It was filed off."

"When did you give it to Lucy?" Cal asked.

"Last time I saw her," he said. "The night before she got killed."

He mopped his eyes with his sleeve, then looked at Cal. His cigarette was burning down between his fingers.

"What am I going to do?"

"I'll take care of you, buddy," Cal said, getting up and taking the cigarette away before it hurt him. "Right now, you'd better try to get to sleep."

He led him into the bedroom. Esther and I sat in

silence for a few minutes, listening to the murmur of their conversation. Hank sounded querulous, Cal reassuring.

"I'm tired," I said.

"Me too."

"It's not even that late," I said, looking at my watch. "It's only nine-thirty."

"It feels like midnight."

"I've been thinking," I began.

"Lucky you. That must mean your brain is still working." she said. "Mine has shut down, fresh out of solutions."

"I think I've figured it out, believe it or not. A lot of things are starting to make sense. But I've got couple of things to check at the players' condo. I can phone Gloves."

"What have you got?" Esther asked, excited. "Come on! We're in this together, right?"

"I'm not sure yet, but I've been thinking about a crying baby and spare keys."

"Huh?"

Cal came out of the bedroom, closing the door behind him.

"He's out for the night," he said. "I'll just stop and speak to Rita on the way and see if she'll check in on him in the morning. I feel kind of guilty leaving him this way."

"I imagine this is a pretty normal night for old Hank," I said. "Come the morning he will probably have forgotten everything."

"Maybe, but I'll still check in on him," Cal said. "Are you two ready to go? I should get home pretty soon."

We turned off the light and left the trailer. Cal

went to the house while we got in the car. The dog barked.

"I've got to get to a phone," I said.

"Let's go back to my place," Esther said.

Cal got into the car and started it up.

"Where to?"

"Esther's," I said. "For now."

"I think Kate has a theory," Esther explained, "but she isn't letting us in on it except by telling me riddles."

"I need to ask a few more questions, first. I have to use her phone."

"Let's go to my place, then. It's closer, and I'd like to see if Beth is okay."

"Good idea," Esther said.

"If you don't think she'll mind," I said. "I'm not sure she needs to have a stranger around right now, though."

"No, really, she's fine," Cal said.

Cal's place was only five minutes away from Hank's trailer, but it might as well have been on another planet. It was a big, rambling house with screened verandas on a large, treed lot. It looked welcoming, with a light burning on the front porch.

Inside, it was my kind of place, cluttered and cosy, full of stuff. Books and magazines were piled on the coffee table, there were paintings and posters on the wall, and curious objects filled all available surfaces. One cabinet was full of old windup toys; a chest held a collection of boxes of various types; straw, carved wood, ceramic, and lacquer; there was a jumble of beautiful baskets in a bay window. The floors were gleaming wood in wide planks, covered here and there with different kinds of rugs, some of them skewed by the excitement of a large dog of no apparent pedigree, who was trying to knock Cal over in welcome. A fat orange-and-white cat sat in the most comfortable-looking armchair and watched us all with feline disdain.

"This is beautiful," I said. "Can I move in tomorrow?"

Cal laughed.

"Any time," he said. "If you can stand the kids and animals. There's a phone in the kitchen. I'll just go check on Beth."

He went up the stairs, softly calling her name. Esther showed me to the kitchen and sat at the table, while I stood at the counter and dialled Gloves's number.

"Am I disturbing you? I know it's late."

"No, everyone's still up," he said.

"Is Axel Bonder around, too?"

"I saw him half an hour ago."

"Good. I may have to come over in a bit to talk to him and some other people. Can I use your place?"

"Sure, why?"

"Put it this way," I said. "If I'm right, Dommy should be in uniform by the weekend."

"You've done it? That's great!"

"Just answer me this," I said. "Who lived in Alex and Dommy's apartment last year?"

He told me.

"I'll be right over," I said, and told him who else to invite.

Cal came into the kitchen as I got off the phone. He was laughing.

"She was in bed," he said. "Reading a book and

246

eating apples and cheese. She isn't worried or mad. She just sent Esther her love and told me to be careful."

"I've just got one more call to make," I said. "What's the number at the police department?"

CHAPTER

36

Cal and Esther asked me questions all the way to Gloves's place, but I wouldn't tell them my theory until I had a few more answers. We waited outside the gate for Troy Barwell to arrive. I didn't want to go in until the whole group was gathered and the police were on the scene. It would be awkward to answer questions beforehand. Besides, why spoil the drama?

"You think it's Barwell?" Esther said. "I like him for it. But I don't know what crying babies have to do with anything."

"I like Bonder," Cal said. "He was hanging around the place all weekend long. He's got the keys. What's to stop him from using them and making the switch?"

"Yeah, but he wouldn't have had sex with her," Esther said. "Come on."

"Maybe the second guy didn't have anything to do with it. Maybe it was the other player, what's his name, the catcher she was after."

The conversation stopped when the Sunland Police Department cruiser pulled up and the three of us got out of the van. Barwell had his sidekick, Sargent, with him, as I had requested.

"I'm here strictly under orders, Ms Henry," he said. "I don't like civilians telling me what to do. But the chief told me to come, so I'm here. Let's get this cockamamie thing over with so I can get back to doing my job."

We went to the Gardiners' door, which Karin opened. Her excitement was obvious.

"They're here, Kate, like you asked."

There were nine people waiting for us, all the ones I had told Gloves to invite. They were crowded into the living room, some on furniture that had been brought in from the patio. Gloves sat on the couch along the wall to my right as I came in the door. Karin and Esther went to join him there.

In the corner between the couch and and the sliding glass patio doors sat Axel Bonder, looking ill at ease, wearing his coveralls. Alex Jones sat on the floor next to him, his back to the doors, looking relaxed and interested.

Stinger Swain and Tracy were side by side on a patio lounge chair, with Goober Grabowski slightly behind them on a dining-room chair. There were two more chairs free for Cal and Barwell, next to Eddie and Clarice Carter along the back wall beside the door. Sargent stood. I crossed to the kitchen entrance.

"I'm trying to refrain from saying that I'm sure you wonder why I asked you all here," I said. Only Gloves and Cal smiled. This was a tough audience.

"Well, it's because I think that the key to Lucy's

murder is right here in this room, and I have a few questions to ask."

"Who do you think you are?" Stinger asked. "No one told me we had to go through this shit."

He started to get up. Tracy put her hand on his arm and looked at him sternly. He sat back down.

"This is horseshit," he said.

"Maybe," I replied. "But you might find it interesting. Stick around and see."

I looked at Bonder, miserable in his corner.

"First of all, Mr. Bonder, I want to ask you a question about something that happened last Sunday afternoon. You were seen coming out of Alex Jones's apartment. Is that correct?"

"Yes, he saw me. Avila."

"Can I ask what you were doing there?"

"Doing my job," he said, slightly belligerently. "I went by and saw the door open. I seen Jones here go out half an hour before, so I checked to make sure everything was all right."

"And was it?"

"I don't know. I called, and there was no answer, so I just closed the door and made sure it was locked. I don't want no trouble."

"Then Mr. Avila came and saw you there."

"Yeah."

"Did he say anything?"

"Asked what I was doing there, same as you," he said.

"And you told him what you just told me?"

"Yeah."

"Thank you. Now, Detective Sergeant Barwell, did you come to the condo that day, Sunday, that is?"

"No, not until the next day."

"To what purpose?"

"To search Domingo Avila's apartment."

"On what grounds?"

"We had information that he was in possession of a gun that could match the ballistics on the murdered girl. We also had learned he was involved with Lucy Cartwright and could have a motive for her murder."

"Mr. Bonder, did Detective Sergeant Barwell come to you with the search warrant on Monday?"

"Yeah. I let him in."

"Was he alone?"

"No. The other guy was with him," he said.

"Detective Sargent?"

"I don't know his name," Bonder said.

"How long would you say they were there?"

"None of my business."

"I'm not asking you to be exact," I said. "But was it two hours? An hour? Just an estimate."

"Not that long."

"Half an hour? Five minutes?"

"About that," Bonder said.

"That was quick, Barwell," I said. "You must have known right where to look. Where did you find it, by the way?"

"In his top dresser drawer."

"Was the ammunition there, too?"

"Yeah, there was a box with it."

I looked at Sargent.

"Were you with him when he found the gun, detective?"

"Actually, no," he said. "I was searching the kitchen."

"And?"

"And he called me and showed me the gun."

"Then you left."

"Of course, Ms Henry," Barwell said. "We wanted to get it to the lab."

"And you went directly to the ballpark, did not pass Go, and arrested Domingo Avila."

"We'd found our guy," he said, smugly.

"Were any fingerprints found on this gun you found so quickly?" I asked.

He shook his head.

"It had been wiped clean."

"How convenient," I said.

"What the hell are you getting at?"

"Take a Valium, Detective Sergeant. I'm getting there."

I turned to Gloves and Karin.

"Let's go back to the night of Lucy's murder," I said. "Gloves, could you please repeat what you told me about the scene at the party between Lucy Cartwright and Stinger Swain."

"Well, Tracy had the baby out and there were a bunch of people around. Lucy was talking to Tracy about her, all that woman stuff, and made some comment about her birthday. The kid had just turned one."

"I think she said that it didn't seem like a year since she was born," Karin interrupted.

"Yeah, that was it," Gloves said. "Anyway, Stinger began yelling at her and telling her to keep away from his kid. I mean, he just lost it."

"We thought he was going to hit her," Karin said. Stinger crossed his arms and glared. Tracy sat calmly, with her hands folded in her lap, looking at Karin, her colour a bit high.

"What happened then?" I asked.

"Goober got Stinger away from there," Karin said. "I took Lucy off to the other side of the pool. I think Tracy went back inside her apartment."

"I put Ashley back to bed," she said.

"And what about you, Stinger? Where did you and Goober go? Do you remember?"

"We went out to the beach," Grabowski said. "I thought he should cool off."

"What was the problem, Stinger?"

"That's private," he said. "It's got nothing to do with anything."

"It's just a coincidence that you became violently enraged with a woman who was found dead a couple of hours later?" I asked.

He didn't say anything.

"Goober, do you know how long you were on the beach?"

"I don't like your attitude," he said. "You're trying to make something out of nothing. Stinger just has a short fuse. You know that. It wasn't half an hour before he'd calmed down and was joking about it. No, more like ten minutes."

"But you and Stinger didn't go back to the party."

"The party was no good. I went back to my place and got a bottle of Cutty and took it out to the beach. Stinger and I had our own party."

"How long did the two of you stay out there drinking?"

"I don't remember. I think I passed out. When I came to I was pretty sick, so I went back to my place. Everyone else had gone to bed."

"What time was it?"

"I can answer that," Karin said. "It was almost

two. I got up to get a glass of ice water from the kitchen, and I heard someone being sick out by the pool. I saw him over by the garden. Then he went to his apartment. Clarice saw him, too."

Eddie's wife nodded in agreement.

"Mr. Bonder, did you see this, too?"

"No, I just cleaned up the mess the next day," he said.

"Thank you. Goober, where was Stinger when you came to?"

"I don't know."

"Stinger?"

"Hey, he passed out on me," Swain said. "I tried to wake him, but he was too far gone. There was no scotch left. I came back here. There was nothing happening, so I went to bed."

"What time?"

"I didn't look at the clock."

"Tracy?"

"I was asleep by midnight," she said. "I didn't hear him come in."

"Of course," I said. "But did you hear him go out?"

She sat, silently, pleading with her eyes.

"Because you did go out again, didn't you?" I asked Stinger. "You decided to go for a swim to clear your head."

"What if I did?"

"So you admit that you went back out?"

He shrugged, but didn't say anything.

"What time was this?"

"What's the big deal? So I went for a swim. It's not against the law."

"All right, Stinger, bear with me here," I said.

"I'm just trying to figure out who was where when Lucy got shot. That was about ten past two, I think. So you left Goober on the beach, went back to your place, changed into your bathing suit, and went out again. We know Goober was up and about by quarter to two. Clarice heard him and noticed the time. So, let's say it was one-thirty when you went for your swim. That would fit."

"Can I ask what the point is you're trying to make," Barwell said. "I've got better things to do with my time."

"I think the point will become obvious. Now, Stinger, did you see anyone while you were swimming?"

"No."

"What about on the way back, just before two?"

"No."

"What about Lucy? That was about the time she was leaving Dommy's place. You didn't see her?"

"I told you I didn't see anyone," he said.

I looked at him. So did everybody else in the room. He glared back defiantly.

"Would you be willing to swear to that?" I asked.

Tracy put her hands to her ears. "Stop it! Shut up!"

"You bitch," Stinger said to me. "You interfering fucking bitch."

Sargent had crossed the room before Stinger was completely on his feet, and grabbed him by the arms before he could get to me. I backed away.

"Let's all calm down here," I said. "I'm not through yet."

CHAPTER

37

Karin got up and went to the kitchen and came back with water for Tracy. Everyone began to talk at once, asking questions.

"Let's just give Tracy time to calm down," I said. "In the meantime, Mr. Bonder, can you tell me how many keys there are to these apartments."

"Depends on how many people are staying there."

"Do any ever go missing?"

"Sometimes," he said.

"And what happens then, you change the locks?"

"No. It's too expensive. We write to the guests and ask them to return them," he said. "If they don't, then we might change them. Depends on who they are. Most of our guests are not dishonest."

"What about last spring?" I asked. "Did you have to write to any of the guests?"

"One," he said. "Mr. Swain forgot to turn his in."

"You were alone here last year, weren't you, Stinger?" I asked. "Tracy was home having Ashley, right? She just had her first birthday. Maybe you'd remind me, Mr. Bonder, which apartment he was living in last year."

"Number six, the one Mr. Jones has this year."

I looked around the room, tempted to milk the scene even more. I could see from the faces that I didn't have to.

"Are you all right, Tracy?" I asked. "Can I go on?"

Her eyes were shut, her lips moving. She might have been praying.

"This is speculation, Detective Sergeant Barwell. I'm only an amateur. But I'm sure you can check it out."

I looked at Stinger again.

"You met up with Lucy after she left Dommy's, didn't you?"

"Fuck off."

"And you convinced her somehow to go for a walk along the beach with you. Lucy was always ready for a lark, wasn't she? Maybe you apologized. You probably bitched about your wife a bit, how cold she had turned since she was born-again."

I turned to talk to the others.

"He didn't realize it, but he pressed one of Lucy's buttons. She had no time for born-agains. She thought they were all hypocrites like her step-father."

I looked back at Swain.

"So you ended up down the beach behind the Gulf Vistas. And you talked her into a quickie for old times' sake."

Stinger looked at Tracy, and put his head in his hands.

"Don't listen to her," he pleaded.

"I don't understand," Karin said. "If she, you know, did what he wanted, why did he kill her?"

"Because he knew she would talk," Alex said. "Then he blamed it on Dommy because he hates Dominicans."

"I'm not through," I said. "I want to go back to the question I asked Tracy a while ago. You said you didn't hear him come in. You were telling the truth. But you heard him go out. Or maybe you just woke up alone and were worried about him. You went to the beach to look for him."

She was praying harder.

I walked over and put my hand on her shoulder. She tensed.

"You found him, didn't you? You saw your husband and Lucy together."

She put her hands over her ears again and bent over with her elbows between her knees and began to make a horrible keening sound.

"And then what happened? You ran back to the apartment and got the gun and loaded it. You heard your baby crying, probably, but you didn't stop to comfort her. I don't know whether you were going to kill him or her or both of them, but it was Lucy you found, still on the deck chair."

I took her shoulder.

"Answer me, Tracy. What happened then?"

She stopped her noises and looked at me.

"She laughed at me," Tracy said, her voice flat and expressionless. "She mocked me and my faith."

She sat up straight and looked around the room, her beautiful face calm. She looked strangely peaceful.

"God will forgive me for what I have done. I have accepted Jesus as my saviour."

She got up and walked to her husband.

"I killed the whore. She will never tempt you again. And now she is burning in Hell. Praise the Lord."

Stinger looked up at her. She touched his face gently, and they looked into each other's eyes. The rest of us were like statues. Then she stepped back from him and turned towards the door.

"Stop her," Barwell said, going for his gun. Sargent grabbed her by the arm.

"There's no need, officer," she said. "I'm just going to say goodbye to my children. You'll have to take care of them by yourself now, my darling."

"I'll go with you," Sargent said.

Stinger stumbled to his feet and followed them.

"Oh, my God," Karin said. "I can't believe this."

"What do you think?" Esther asked. "Did he know she did it?"

"Maybe. He must have suspected," I said. "I assume he was in the water when it happened. Lucy was waiting with his towel. Either he saw it happen, or he heard the shot, or just found Lucy afterwards and guessed."

"So he planted the gun?" Gloves asked.

"I don't know. That's for the police to figure out."

I turned to Barwell again.

"If you check with the police in Georgia where he comes from, you'll probably find that he has an ownership permit for a Police Special. And I don't think he'll be able to produce the gun. Captain Marshall over at the A-1 Veteran's probably sold him the ammunition."

"Why didn't she just get rid of the gun?" Gloves said. "Why frame Dommy?"

"I'm not sure," I said. "Only she knows, but I would guess that she thought if they had another suspect they wouldn't look any further. She had the key to Dommy's place and she had seen that his gun was just like theirs. With or without Stinger's help, she realized that she could get rid of the gun and frame Dommy at the same time. He meant nothing to her. So she filed off the numbers and made the switch. The file might even be in their apartment, or a hardware store clerk will remember selling it."

"Do you think it was Stinger who phoned you with that threat earlier?" Esther asked.

"It could have been. But it could have been Tracy, too. The voice was disguised."

I went and collected my purse.

"You'll be making the arrest tonight?"

Barwell nodded.

"Then I'm off. It's late. I'll come by in the morning to make a statement."

He started to speak.

"I'll be there first thing," I said. "This time I promise. If you promise me something else."

"What?"

"Just get Dommy's ass out of jail."

Everyone was standing. Alex came across the room to me.

"Thank you," he said, tears in his eyes. I hugged him. And Gloves and Karin and Eddie and Clarice. I stopped when I got to Bonder, and stuck out my hand.

"Thank you for your help," I said.

He took my hand and nodded. I went to the door.

"Cal, can you give me a ride home? I've got a story to write."

We rode for a while in silence. Esther broke it.

"How did you figure it out?"

"I'd been looking at Stinger as the one," I said. "He didn't seem to be able to account for the relevant times. I knew he had a gun. I just couldn't figure out how to prove it.

"Then this afternoon when Clarice told me about hearing a baby crying for quite a while, I began to wonder why."

"What made you think it was the Swain baby?" Cal asked.

"I wasn't sure. But it could have been. And one reason she would have kept on crying was if there was no one there to comfort her."

"So you figured that Tracy had to be missing too."

"Yeah. Then I began to see the picture. All I had to do was figure out how she made the switch."

"Or how he did," Cal said.

"Whatever."

"Why don't I feel better about this?" Esther asked.

"Well, when I think about Dommy, I feel pretty good," I said. "But when I think about Tracy, or even Stinger, I feel like I've just destroyed their lives. And the kids, what about them? No, I don't feel very good either."

"Yeah, I know what you mean," Cal said. "I don't think I'll give up my day job and go in for detecting."

When they dropped me at my hotel, we agreed to get together in a few days when we felt more like celebrating. I called the office and dictated a short story. It was on deadline, so they couldn't take more than that. I promised more in the morning. Then I called Andy and woke him up.

"Well, I did it," I said.

"Good for you! Who was it?"

"Stinger's wife killed the whore. In her words."

"You sound down."

"I am."

"It's a normal reaction. Part of it is just the letdown from all that adrenalin you've been pumping out over the last few days. And it's made worse because you know the people involved."

"Yeah."

"It happens to me all the time. We just made an arrest in the hooker case I told you about. He was seventeen, an addict, but just a kid. I don't feel great about putting him away either."

"I guess you can't come down and visit again."

"I've been back for, what, three and a half days?"

"Yeah, I know."

"Just get some sleep. I'll talk to you tomorrow."

"Okay. And, Andy?"

"What, love?"

"Remind me to stick to reporting next time?"

"Yeah, sure. And you'll listen, right?"

CHAPTER

38

A couple of days later, I had good reason to feel better, looking across the table at Dommy Avila's smiling face. We were at Molly's for a celebration of his release from jail. There were four pitchers of beer laid out down the long table, which was covered with newspapers to catch the debris from six heaping platters of shrimp.

It was June Hoving's idea that we come here. I went to her house the day after Tracy was arrested to return Lucy's picture and tell her about it. She had decided to go back to work, and said she wanted to see Dommy and apologize for the way he had been treated. She liked the idea of a party at her restaurant. He was Lucy's friend, after all.

"Hey, Kate, no food like this in the jail, man," Dommy said, his accent thick. "I was hungry in there."

"Eat, Dommy, eat," said Esther Hirsch, then laughed. "God, I sound like my mother."

It was a large and raucous crowd. Cal was there with Beth, the Gardiners, Alex Jones, Tiny Washington, Eddie and Clarice Carter, Joe Kelsey, Atsuo Watanabe, Flakey Patterson, Bony Costello, and Jeff Glebe. Others had promised to join us later.

I had spent Friday writing two stories, one on Tracy and Stinger's arrest and the other, longer, feature on Lucy. I hoped that I had done justice to her.

"You're pretty quiet," Jeff said.

"I'm just thinking that I wished I had known Lucy better," I said. "I might have been able to prevent all of this."

He cocked his eyebrow.

"You're taking yourself too seriously again," he said.

"Well, maybe if I had taken her more seriously, she wouldn't have needed to find her approval through sex."

"You really believe that?"

I shook my head.

"No, I don't. But I wish I hadn't just brushed her off all the time. I never looked beyond her clothes and hair and big tits. She was interesting, Jeff, really."

"If you say so. But you're being a drag on the party. Lighten up."

He poured me a glass of beer.

"And that's an order."

"Aye-aye, sir," I said. We clinked glasses. Avila reached across with his glass and joined us.

"To friends," he said. "To my very good friend Kate."

"And to you, Dommy. Welcome back."

Glasses were raised all around the table.

"Hey, Kate," Gloves yelled. "Did Dommy tell you

what happened when he got to the ballpark after he got out of jail?"

"No," I said. Dommy shook his head and laughed.

"Skipper made him stay an hour late running laps."

"He say I am behind in my training," Dommy said. "Yesterday, two hours he hit fungoes to me. But he no extra BP."

Everybody laughed.

"Batting practice is fun, Dommy," Joe Kelsey said. "You don't get to have fun yet."

"Man, he is one tough skipper," Dommy said. "I think jail easier except the food, it was *bad*."

He attacked the shrimps again. I turned to Cal, who was sitting on my left. Beth, on his other side, was laughing with Tiny Washington.

"Did you go see Hank on Friday?" I asked Cal.

"Yeah. He was in pretty rough shape. But he asked me to help him get into the dry-out clinic. He's going to try to give up the booze."

"And drugs?"

"Come on, he'll never give up his weed. But that's not what's killing him."

"So, did you have any luck with the clinic?"

"He's there as we speak."

"How can he afford it?"

"He can't," Cal said.

"So?"

"So, I can," he shrugged. "I told him I'd give him a job when he gets out and he can pay me back."

"Do you think he'll stick it out?"

"I'm not counting on it," he said. "But he's never even got this far before. Who knows?"

"That's very generous of you."

"And of Beth," he reminded me, taking her hand. She looked at him, surprised.

"I'm telling Kate about Hank," he explained to her.

"There but for the grace of God," she said.

"Yeah, there's some of that," he admitted. "I probably should have helped him out a lot sooner."

"There's lots of things we all should do that we don't," I said. "We can't beat ourselves up over them."

"No, I guess not. I don't know how much my motivation for all of this has to do with what I now know about Lucy, and how much is just because I feel like Hank deserves a break, another chance."

"It's probably a bit of both," I said. "But there's nothing wrong with that. The important thing is that you are helping him."

"I'm never going to tell him, you know."

"I didn't think you would."

"It's going to be tough to keep it to myself," he said.

"The toughest," I agreed. "Especially as you spend more time with him. Anyway, I hope he makes it. Maybe that talent hasn't been completely lost after all."

"Yeah, here's hoping," he said.

I excused myself and found the ladies' room. Esther came in a few minutes later. We talked from adjoining cubicles.

"What's new?" I asked.

"I had a call from a prospective client," she said. "Tracy Swain."

"You're kidding! Are you defending her?"

"No, it would be a conflict of interest, much as I'd like to. I referred her to another good lawyer instead."

"But she's guilty."

"Guilty of something, sure, but that doesn't mean she doesn't deserve a good defence. I don't want to see her go down for first-degree murder. There's capital punishment in Florida, remember."

I flushed the toilet and went to the sink.

"I don't know how you do your job," I said. "Doesn't it depress you?"

"Sometimes. Doesn't yours?" She flushed. I waited.

"Yeah," I said, after, "but the worst thing that can happen to the guys I deal with is they get sent to the minors."

"There is that," she said, coming out of her cubicle.

"What about Stinger? They let him out on bail."

"It's not as serious a charge."

"He's the real villain here," I said.

"You could say that," she agreed. "So what's he doing?"

"The team has given him time off to deal with things. He has the kids, for one thing. Besides, who wants him around?"

"Do you think he'll play again if he gets acquitted?"

"Is that likely to happen?"

"From what I hear, they haven't got any hard evidence on him," Esther said. "He could have been unaware of what she had done. Innocent until proven guilty, you know."

"I can't imagine him playing with the Titans again. But stranger things have happened in baseball."

"But they'll keep paying him, won't they?"

"What, are you worried about your friend's fees?"

"No," she laughed. "I was just thinking how ironic it is. Here's the one true bad guy in the whole thing, and he sits at home and gets paid, what, a thousand a day?"

"Stinger? No. He's a million-a-year guy. I figured it out once. I think the figure turned out to be something like two thousand, seven hundred, and forty dollars a day, give or take some small change. That's every day, Sundays and holidays included. Slightly less in leap year."

"Beats working for a living," she said.

"Well, he can certainly afford a lawyer."

"Lucky for him," she said, holding the door for me.

Esther went back to the table. I stopped at the bar.

"Hi, June, how are you doing?"

She smiled, looking surprisingly perked up.

"It's good to be back at work," she said. "And it's good to see you guys having fun."

"It's not bothering you?"

"Dommy's a nice kid. I always thought so. I'm glad it wasn't him."

"It's a slow night. Do you want to come join us?"

She shook her head and brushed the hair off her forehead.

"I don't think I'm quite ready for that," she said. "But thanks. And I'd like to see you again before you go back."

"I would, too. I'll call."

"Thanks," she said. "And thanks for what you did. I appreciate it."

I went back to the table and sat down. They were talking baseball. What else is new?

It was a good night. I left, a bit foggy, before the rest. I was heading towards my car when I heard a honk. It was Troy Barwell in his cruiser.

"I wouldn't get in that car if I were you," he said. "You're in no condition. I'd have to arrest you."

"You're right, of course. But did you ever try to find a taxi around here?"

"I'm it," he said. "Get in."

I did.

"Good party?" he asked.

"The best," I said.

We drove the few minutes to my hotel in silence. When I was getting out of the car he stopped me.

"I should apologize," he said. "And thank you."

"Oh, okay," I said. " I didn't mean to meddle in your business. I just had a story to write."

I opened the door.

"Good night," he said.

I paused, with my hand on the door, then closed it and leaned back into the window.

"Hey, we're all on the same side," I said. "Right, Detective Sergeant Teensy?"

He peeled away so fast he almost took my hand off. Suddenly, I felt like a million bucks.